PRAISE FOR *Grave Disturbance*

A taut and intelligent whodunit, Crites' first book thrives on its grim Northwestern atmosphere and dark contemporary themes. A sharply written mystery introducing a new detective with a lot of promise.

Kirkus

Beautifully written, *Grave Disturbance* evokes the fragile beauty of the Cascades foothills and the precarious balance of the human mind in the grip of fear. The story feels so real you can smell the dirt from the plundered graves.

Jeanne Matthews, author of *Where the Bones Are Buried*, a Dinah Pelerin mystery

An atmospheric mystery novel filled with lyrical language that will transport you to a misty place where nothing is clear and danger hides in the shadows. Follow Grace Vaccaro, an empathetic and unflappable mental health professional, through the rain-splattered streets of Seattle to the eastern exurbs where developers, native tribes and her own neighbors struggle to keep their pieces of the Pacific Northwest for themselves. A box of human bones, the disjointed ranting of a mentally impaired woman and two seemingly unrelated murders are the puzzle pieces that Grace must put together to prevent more deaths.

Rachel Bukey, author of *Leap of Faith*, an Anne Dexter mystery

Grave Disturbance

By Martha Crites

Grave Disturbance

Martha Crites

Rat City Publishing

Seattle

Copyright © 2015 by Martha Crites

First print edition: December 2015
ISBN 978-0-9835714-1-4

Cover by Aaron Weholt

Interior Design by Waverly Fitzgerald

Published by Rat City Publishing
www.RatCityPublishing.com

Dedication

For Jim—you are a saint

Chapter 1

THE SOUND OF MY HEELS echoed on the hard tile floor in the basement passageway. Overhead, asbestos-wrapped pipes and bunched electrical wires hung exposed from the low ceiling. It was midnight and I'd just finished an evening shift. My work had brought me to Harborview, Seattle's old county hospital, for nearly twenty years. But I had never been to the morgue.

A tall woman with cropped brown hair answered the door to the medical examiner's office and listened to my request. "I'm sorry. We don't have people identify bodies anymore." She gripped the doorknob in one hand, the frame in the other and waited for me to leave.

"When I called earlier, they said there could be a match. The man I'm looking for is Martin Hanish. He's sixty-two—"

"It's too hard on people. We confirm identities scientifically these days—fingerprints, dental records." Her voice was patient, as if she had explained this a hundred times. Behind her, a water cooler floated a stream of bubbles through its upside-down blue plastic bottle.

I reached in my pocket and pulled out my ID. Usually I kept it hidden, but tonight I wanted to take advantage of any professional courtesy that might come my way. The woman and I weren't in the same discipline. I evaluated people with serious mental illness for involuntary psychiatric treatment, but I knew a camaraderie existed among the people who take care of Seattle's daily tragedies: the cops, firefighters, mental health professionals and, I hoped, the investigators at the medical examiner's office.

"My name is Grace Vaccaro. The woman I talked to earlier said they hadn't come up with a fingerprint match. I'm concerned about the family. His sister can be fragile . . . "

I left it vague enough to sound job related, but the trip was personal. Martin's sister was my best friend. I'd triggered Gwen's panic when I called that morning to ask if she'd heard from him in the last few days. "He's about five-eight and thin, has short ,gray hair. I'm sure it's not him," I said. "But the family would be so relieved—"

"Enough." She eyed my name tag with ambivalence and swung the door open. "I'm Donna Gloss. The description does sound like a match for a Doe that came in tonight." She ran her finger down a list that used the military alphabet to name the unidentified bodies and stopped at Echo Doe. "You wait there." She pointed to a tiny room where a couch upholstered in institutional green faced an interior window. The dim waiting area could have belonged to any doctor's office after hours— except for the smell. Disinfectant couldn't mask the odor of death.

A bank of white mini-blinds blocked the view into the space where Echo Doe, who might or might not be Martin, was about to be displayed. I'd never been the squeamish type, but the task and the smell and the hour combined to give me a sense of unreality.

Metal wheels squeaked behind the wall. Donna Gloss rejoined me in the darkened viewing area. She looked like an athlete but folded her hands in front of her as if she were waiting for a classroom to settle down before she addressed it.

"Have you seen someone dead before?"

"Not like this."

I sat up straight on the couch and wondered what drove me to take on the search. In another day or two, dental records would have done the job anyway. But I couldn't wait. Gwen was the kind of person whose emotions percolated close to the sur- face. If Martin was dead, she needed to know, not jump in anticipation every time the phone rang.

"I'm afraid the body is in bad shape," Donna said.

Bright light from the other room leaked through the edge of the blinds and my eyes welled with held-back tears. The clinical

2

atmosphere of the medical examiner's office made me want to tell this woman that if it was Martin, he wasn't just a body; he was a person with a life.

"He lives out in the Snoqualmie Valley and just retired from the University. He started a film business," I said. "His dream."

"It's not fair, I know." She tapped the clear plastic wand that would open the blinds but let it drop again. "Are you sure you want to do this?"

I told myself I was doing it for Gwen. I'm good at taking care of people. My practice began at my mother's knee. She suffered from a serious depression long before the invention of antidepressants. When she was too debilitated to take care of me, which was much of the time, I took care of her. I stepped closer to the window and rested my fingers on the sill. "I'm ready."

The woman opened the blinds to reveal a covered figure on a stainless steel gurney. The form beneath the sheet seemed weightless, diminished. White tiles and deep sinks glinted under harsh fluorescent tubes. She hurried to the other side of the wall and caught my eye through the window.

I nodded.

She pulled back the sheet, exposing the top half of his face, broken and misshapen, and then the rest. Chalky skin, discolored into a purple bruise. Dull clumps of gray hair matted with blood. The frail-looking cheekbones seemed to have crumbled under his unruly eyebrows. A face I had seen just days ago. I clutched the wall in front of me.

It wasn't Martin.

Chapter 2

I CLOSED MY EYES and wished I could rewind the last sixteen hours—back to where I woke up in bed, warm under the down comforter. But the morning seemed to have other plans.

I'd gone about my usual routine: started the coffee, grabbed my raincoat and sprinted through a relentless March drizzle to let the chickens out to range free. Back in the house, I hung my wet coat on a peg by the back door and stole a cup of coffee from the pot while it was still brewing. A film of condensation fogged the window over the kitchen sink. I wiped it away and watched the rain, glad to be inside. The chickens congregated under the shelter of an old cedar to avoid the downpour.

The rainfall here in the foothills of the Cascade Mountains was double that of Seattle, thirty miles to the west. Protected from the deluge, the chickens puffed out their feathers and scratched themselves with their long pink bird feet. The rooster, red with glossy green tail feathers, strutted and clucked for the hens each time he found a worm.

I left the window and sat down to write an email to my daughter, Nell, who was studying Spanish in Guadalajara for a semester. Our relationship had been chilly since before she left. I'd hoped the distance would provide a buffer. She needed independence and I needed to let her go. But her last email was a tirade—I had called too early in the morning and made her late for class. A simple, "Got to go, Mom," at the time wouldn't do. I stared at the blinking cursor on the Blueberry iMac Nell had insisted I buy. We were just starting the twenty-first century after all, and I had been slow to get my first computer.

A frenzy of squawking started outside. "Grace!" My husband, Frank, called from the upstairs bedroom. "What's wrong with the chickens?"

I grabbed my raincoat and ran out the door toward the noise in the overgrown orchard behind the house.

"It's Martin's goddamn dog again," Frank shouted from the window. The "goddamn dog" was a four-month-old husky who had already killed my favorite chicken. The hens flapped and scattered, and the screeching rooster sped into a patch of brambles with the dog close behind.

"Caesar, stop," I ordered the dog. But by the time I reached them, the rooster had disappeared and the young dog crouched, mouth full of feathers, his soft, gray puppy fur wet and coated with mud. He puffed out clouds of steam in the chilly air. I grabbed his collar to prevent further carnage.

Frank was outside by then, his shirt half buttoned. "I'll find the rooster." He surveyed the sea of blackberry bushes. Long canes twisted into an impenetrable front.

I nodded toward the path that ran through the woods between our two houses. "I'll take Caesar home."

"Tell Martin that if he doesn't keep his dog tied up, I will." Frank's face had aged into crags and angles amplified by a thick mustache, the kind of face that frightened me as a little girl. Now his solidity reassured me. I kissed him as well as I could while bending over with my hand on the dog's collar. We wouldn't see each other again until after midnight. Frank was remodeling a house near Lake Joy and his hours were long and could be unpredictable. I was scheduled on the three to eleven shift in Seattle.

"Leave me a note," he said. "I'll probably be gone when you get back."

I maneuvered the dog past the cottage with its deck that jutted over a shallow pond. Frank had built the cottage as a guest house shortly after we moved in and turned it over to Nell when she was fifteen. He negotiated the push and pull of our daughter's growing-up better than I did. Nell and I were probably too much alike. We both had the same dark hair and broad-shouldered stature—and a stubbornness that kept us in conflict. The cottage windows reflected the gray sky and water.

The way to Martin's skirted the pond, then entered the woods on a muddy trail. Vine maples covered in dripping moss vaulted the path and clumps of sword fern grew to prehistoric proportions. I bent under the bowed branches and pulled the puppy behind me. Caesar held his front legs out straight and put on the brakes. He knew he was in trouble.

"Come on, Caesar. You look like you've been out all night." The puppy forgot he was in trouble and trotted beside me. I was angry about my rooster, but Martin had been a friend for years. In the clearing, his house, rustic and hand-built, sat beyond the wide lawn. Like a lot of people in the foothills, he used a wood stove as his only source of heat, but no smoke curled from the chimney this morning.

"Martin?" I knocked and called his name, knocked again. I touched the knob; his door was unlocked as usual. Any other day, I would have walked right in, but this time I eased the door open a few inches, then hesitated. The house was too quiet.

Caesar pushed through the opening, ears flattened. Dogs know when something is wrong. I rushed ahead, afraid Martin might be ill. Two steps in I saw the chaos. The house was ransacked. Drawers dumped, their contents heaped on the floor amid broken glass from lamps and picture frames. The house was silent except for the tick of the cuckoo clock, slow and insistent as a heartbeat. I froze in the entryway before I forced myself to check each room. No Martin. Then I pulled Caesar out behind me and ran for home.

The images of willful destruction haunted me. The television lay on the floor, its cracked screen gaping at the ceiling. Discs and camera equipment lay mingled nearby. Signs added up: the dank air, already musty without a fire, the dog left out to roam. Martin hadn't been home all night.

I retraced my steps, imagining Martin lying somewhere, broken too, a victim of the same irrational hand. I tripped over a jagged root and landed on my hands and knees, the wind knocked out of me. Caesar stuck his face in mine and panted hot breath. I pulled myself up and made it home, where all my rushing came to an end when I dialed 911.

The police were backed up. What they considered a burglary, not in progress, wasn't a priority. I couldn't stop thinking, and each scenario I imagined was worse. An angry assault, Martin hurt. I needed to know where he was, that he was okay, but the police still hadn't come when I had to leave for work.

I scrawled a note to Frank and fixed Caesar a bed in the garage. In my job, I dealt with crises all the time, but my worry superseded that. My work suffered that evening. I couldn't concentrate on evaluations. Instead, I phoned hospitals, police, anyone I could think of—until a social worker in the emergency room told me about the unidentified body pulled from a tangle of underbrush by the Snoqualmie River. She delicately suggested I try the morgue.

~

"How do you know him?" Donna Gloss raised her voice to be heard through the autopsy room Plexiglas. She seemed excited by the identification and leaned in for a closer look at the battered face.

I couldn't imagine the mindless fury it must have taken to strike him over and over. And I couldn't lift my eyes from his exposed face. My voice sounded too loud when I called back. "He's homeless. I evaluated him the day before yesterday."

Donna moved around the gurney and pulled back the cover at his side to show a crabbed hand with split and blackened fingernails. "He looks like he might have lived on the streets. I should have told you that in the beginning. What's his name?"

"Alfred Mallecke." I sat down to steady myself. The police report said he had been found at the Pike Place Market, talking back to his voices. That, in itself, wasn't so unusual. You could see it in any large city. The market vendors carried on in spite of him, hawking fish and throwing twenty-pound salmon to impress the tourists. They didn't call the cops until he bit the head off a live pigeon.

They sent him to Harborview for a psychiatric evaluation. When I interviewed Mr. Mallecke, he was psychotic, but not violent—except to pigeons. Not suicidal, not homicidal. He agreed to a next day appointment and medications. I didn't commit him. Now I agonized over my assessment, afraid I had missed a piece of law that would have let me hold him.

Donna snapped off her latex gloves and washed her hands before she returned to the viewing room. "Why didn't you hospitalize him?"

"I wish I could have, but the courts have tightened up on the evidence they'll accept for commitment. People we would have detained in the past, we have to let go." I closed my eyes and tried to visualize him safe on the psychiatric unit, but the rooms and the bedding there were white like the autopsy room. I couldn't wipe away the image of Alfred Mallecke covered again to the top of his head in a sheet that sloped away like a snowfield.

Donna straightened up a notch to what looked like a full six feet. She seemed to realize that I was having a hard time. She'd predicted it. My handwriting crimped on the form she gave me to fill out and the flat, sweet smell of decay clung in my throat.

"We just had a homeless bashing," she said. "A man set up camp near the freeway. Teenagers beat him and left him to die. It could have been one of those."

"I read about that one, but it doesn't fit," I said. "The Snoqualmie River is thirty miles away. I haven't heard of an encampment there. But Martin lived in that area."

"That's why I thought we had a match."

"This guy hung out in downtown Seattle."

Donna drummed her fingers silently on the counter, touching only the fleshy pads to the surface, as if she'd decided not to disturb the quiet now that our task was done.

She motioned me to follow her through a maze of offices. I said good-bye at the door that would release me from the

medical examiners suite and walked into the basement passageway. A guilty part of me rejoiced that I hadn't found
Martin.

~

My old Toyota truck was the only vehicle left on the lower level
of the parking garage. The radio came on when I started it up
and a talk show host spewed a hateful commentary on the dirty
vagrants who littered our streets. As if they weren't human. I
snapped it off. Maybe the woman at the morgue was right. A
homeless bashing could happen anywhere.

I needed some air and rolled down the window when I
reached the ramp that led out of the parking garage. The wind
carried a briny scent from the Puget Sound half a mile down-
hill. The muscles in my shoulders had hardened into painful
knots, and I couldn't get away fast enough. I accelerated past
the brick façade of the old art deco style hospital and flew down
James Street hill onto the freeway. With no traffic to impede
me at that late hour, I sped across Lake Washington on the 520
floating bridge.

Most nights, the tension of the job fell away with each mile
when I left the city for the rainy foothills. My home life provided the calm and balance to the tragedy of broken lives I saw
at work each day. Now I'd lost that balance.

When I was younger, I saw myself as a hotshot advocate for
the civil rights of people with mental illness. But after so many
years, I had seen the results of the occasional bad call by a
mental health professional, or the court: a successful suicide, a
family killed by their son whose voices told him they were
conspiring against him. Now I wished I could round up all the
suffering people and herd them into the hospital where they'd
be okay, but it didn't work that way. The legal system was designed to protect them from impulses like mine.

The night turned blacker in the valley. Mist coated the
windshield. On Mountain View Road, red and blue reflectors

marked the hairpin curve. Martin's place was third on the right, then came mine.

I slammed on my brakes at Martin's mailbox. The house wasn't visible from the road, but a different set of red and blue lights flashed through the naked alders. I forgot about going home and spun gravel up the driveway to his house where two police cars angled in the turnaround. Their lights threw grotesque shadows from the winter-beaten shrub row. Frank was already there and ran to meet me with the puppy on a short leash. His face was pale in the blue light. This was about more than burglary.

"Tell me," I said.

"Martin is dead."

I doubled over as if I'd been hit. I probably imagined it, but the smell of the morgue came back, clinging to my clothing and my hair. I'd been afraid of this news all day. Finally hearing it was too much.

Frank put a hand on my shoulder. "A guy was running down by the river. His dog found him."

I pulled myself up straight and focused on my breathing until a wave of nausea passed. "What happened?"

"They aren't saying much, but I heard he was beaten to death." He paused, "Bludgeoned."

I had seen Mallecke's injuries. I knew what bludgeoned looked like. Martin had been in the same place, probably suffered the same blows. "Does Gwen know?"

"She's on her way."

"God, she'll be devastated." Martin was Gwen's only family.

The mist turned to full-out rain. Frank and I moved up to the deep front porch where we could talk. Martin's front door stood ajar and inside, uniformed officers took pictures and dusted for fingerprints.

A bone-deep chill ran through me. We pressed together to keep warm, or maybe for solace. Frank took a seat on the edge of a planter where last year's annuals had turned to dried twigs. Caesar bumped him with his nose and took Frank's wrist in his jaws with a soft grip that I'd heard was a dominance gesture. Frank peeled the dog off his arm and found a piece of firewood for him to chew on.

"The rooster is okay," he said.

"What?" The chickens were the furthest thing from my mind.

"Caesar only got his tail. He's bloody, but he'll be okay."

"Oh." I saw the strain in Frank's face. Gravity pulled at the laugh lines carved in his cheeks. I stood beside him and rubbed his neck.

"The rooster saved the hens by leading the dog away," he said. "They do that. Put themselves in danger to protect the flock."

"And into the brambles to save himself." All I could think was that Martin hadn't been so lucky.

The sound of tires on the driveway tore through the night. Gwen's old Volvo ground to a stop behind my truck. She threw open the car door and ran up the uneven walk. I met her on the steps. Her henna-red hair seemed garish against the dark landscape. She threw her head back and let the rain wash over her. Her voice rose in a primitive wail. I reached out. She seemed fragile and her shoulder blades trembled like birds' wings when I guided her up the final steps.

"Oh, Grace, I can't believe he's dead." She cried so hard she hyperventilated and her words came out in gasps.

"I'm sorry," I said, helpless to spare her this pain. Gwen was in her fifties, ten years older than I was, but her look was young and flamboyant. The wind picked up her fuchsia kimono and snapped the silk around a lemon yellow mini-skirt that hugged her thighs. She looked like a waif playing dress-up. All I could do was hold on to her.

The sergeant in charge stepped out and cleared his throat to get our attention. Carl Ring's meaty build made him look like a giant next to Gwen. He gave her an awkward pat.

"It's a damned shame," he said. His expression moved from a polite smile to a frown on his doughy face, then back again.

The other officers carried the big silver evidence cases back to the patrol cars and gave us a wide berth when they passed.

"They're almost done now," Carl said. "Did Martin have a computer in there?"

"Of course," Gwen said.

"That's one thing that seems to be missing. Call a list in to the station if you notice more. You can clean up the house when you're ready."

Gwen's voice rose an octave in response. "What do you mean clean up the house? It's a murder scene."

"He wasn't killed in there."

"How do you know? There could be something important."

Carl didn't respond right away. His silence expanded the feeling of unreality I'd had all evening. He finally answered, "We got pictures of everything. You come on down to the station tomorrow, Gwen. We'll talk."

He gave her another pat and nodded to the house. "You'll want to lock it up," he said then headed down the gravel path with a heavy step. We watched until the police cars disappeared down the long driveway and left us in darkness except for a single light on the porch.

Gwen pulled out a cigarette with shaking fingers. The match flared and the familiar smell of her French tobacco gathered under the covered porch. The smoke didn't calm her. "How am I going to lock it up? I don't have keys."

"Martin kept a set in the shed for when he went away," Frank said. His voice trailed off as if he didn't want to bring up the reminder of how very long Martin would be away now.

I found a flashlight in my truck and led the way to the shed. Now that the police were gone, we let Caesar off the leash. He ran in tight circles, wild with pent-up energy. Frank opened the door and felt for the key on a cluttered shelf inside. Caesar pushed in behind him and sniffed in the black interior. I didn't know what Martin kept in there, but I worried about the dog wandering into a tray of rat poison. I reached for his collar, but he moved too fast. He grabbed something and ran out.

"What's he got?" I swung the flashlight in Caesar's direction. Beads of rain sparkled on his fur when the beam swept over him. He mouthed a bone.

"Drop it," I said and reached for the dog. He let me collar him this time. I pressed into the hinges of his jaw to make him release. "He got this from the shed?"

I pulled away a sturdy two-foot bone. It wasn't like the delicate remains of the yearling deer that the dogs drag out from the woods after a cold spell. I aimed the flashlight into the shed. Inside, a cardboard box overflowed with mud-crusted bones. The light threw them into high relief and shadows loomed from behind.

Chapter 3

FRANK SQUEEZED INTO THE NARROW SHED and pulled out the box before it occurred to any of us that we should save it for the police. Rain spattered and made rivulets of mud on the dried-out bones. "Wait," I said too late. "We should leave it there."

Gwen pulled the box out further and angrily mimicked Carl's voice, "It's not a crime scene."

We carried the box up to the porch before the rain made it worse. Gwen waved us inside and turned on the lights, then gasped when she saw what had happened in Martin's house. The mess seemed more hideous than it had in the morning, with a film of fingerprint powder on every surface. I pushed aside the scattered papers and remnants of the burglary to make room for the box on the floor in the entryway.

The box drew our attention. The largest bones reminded me of what I'd learned in junior high science class: tibia, fibula. Tiny fissures were embedded with soil. Frank leaned close and moved them aside, revealing a skull. It was human. "These look old," he said. "Do you think they're Native American?"

"Why would Martin have them?" I said and squatted on my heels. "He could have found them on the property, but everybody knows you have to notify some kind of authorities. The water department discovered a whole village when they excavated for the treatment plant on the Tolt River."

Gwen finally spoke. "Martin was talking to the Snoqualmie Tribe about local archaeology. It was research for a film for the historical society. That's all."

I knew about the film. Martin had given me a copy a couple of days ago when he finished it, but I'd never had time to watch. Now I felt like I'd let him down. "Bones would be revered though. I'm afraid Martin was into something he shouldn't have been."

Gwen paced the floor between the kitchen and the living room with an energy that bordered on mania. "No." She veered around the spilled books and camera equipment, then returned to her track. "Martin was always the responsible one. I ran away, got in trouble. You name it. He cleaned up my messes."

I shoved the broken TV from her path, "I know, but we should let the police know about these. It might have something to do with his murder."

"Stop." She spun to face me. "You make it sound like it's Martin's fault someone killed him."

"I'm sorry. I'm just trying to make sense of it." I reached for her, but she pulled away.

Gwen wasn't ready to calm down. She dropped to her knees and tore through a pile of papers. "Why would they wreck his house?"

In a strange way, the destruction of the house seemed more real to me than Martin's death. This I could see, but I still imagined Martin walking in to survey the damage. Gwen held papers out in crumpled bunches of three or four, looking for the answer. She threw each handful aside until she was just shuffling them on the floor around her and crying.

I'd known Gwen since I was ten and she was my babysitter. She combed my hair, spoke to me in French and told me about her boyfriends. I idolized her. Now I knelt down and she finally let me wrap my arms around her. We rocked back and forth until her sobs quieted to jagged breaths. Sometimes I envied Gwen's expressive nature. Her feelings flashed. Mine were neat and tidy, underground. I was just the person to have around in an emergency, but I wished I could cry too..

"It's late," I said. "Stay with us tonight."

The puppy sensed Gwen's distress and nuzzled her. She leaned back and ruffled his muddy fur. It seemed to pull her out of herself.

"I'll be fine. I want to be alone." She wiped her face on the sleeve of her kimono.

"Why don't you take Caesar with you." I'd seen how the puppy had been a comfort to her. "It'll help."

"Okay. I'll take him. And I'll take the damned bones when I go to the police station in the morning."

Frank and I walked her down to her car and put the box of bones in the big trunk of the Volvo. We watched her drive away, then went back to find the keys we'd forgotten in the shed.

~

Sleep was a relief. Until four-thirty. I dreamed I was climbing in the mountains with Martin. He was alive. I belayed him and fed out the rope in increments when he moved. He climbed with the finesse of a younger man. A bright blue sky backed the scene and my spirits soared to see him like that. Then I watched in shock as he tumbled from the rock face and fell from sight. Before I could save him, the rope snaked through my hands, burning them. I jerked awake, my heart racing.

Frank snored. His arm circled me and rested on my belly. Waves of heat radiated from his body. I threw off the covers to cool down and tried to go back to sleep. The lead-paned window over the dresser framed a pale quarter moon. Outside, a single car passed by. Its tires splashed on the still wet road. I had never given a thought to who might be out this time of night. People work odd hours. They stay late with friends. Maybe they ransack houses and commit murder. I reached for the comforter again.

I thought about Martin, how he used to wander over on summer evenings when he heard our voices through the woods. He always had a magic trick for Nell when she was little. God, I would have to tell Nell. Martin was like family to her. In recent years, if I couldn't find her, I knew she would be at his house, poring over film books or watching old movies on TV.

I worried about calling her too early. She'd be angry, but it was the only way I could be sure of reaching her before she left for class. By the time I got home from work it would be too late.

At five o'clock, the moon dropped to the far corner of the window, about to disappear. I pulled myself out of bed and busied myself with chores. I made dinner ahead for the evening and carried the scraps out to the chickens. They jockeyed for the best position and fell on the vegetable peelings as if they were starving. The rooster looked unbalanced without his plume of tail, but his chivalry was intact. He stood back to let the girls eat first.

Six o'clock, two hours later in Guadalajara. Time to call Nell and make her late for class again. I dialed the country code, city code and phone number of the family she was staying with. Their little girl answered with her clear child's voice. It didn't matter if she understood my halting Spanish, she knew it was the American mom.

"Yes." Nell was curt.

"I'm sorry to call you so early—"

"Not sorry enough," she said. The resentment in her voice carried the two thousand miles quite distinctly. After all, hadn't she just asked me not to bother her early in the morning?

I sat down at the kitchen table and traced the grain in the dark, stained oak. "Martin died yesterday," I told her without preamble.

"Oh no! What happened?" The hostility slid from her voice and she sounded as young as the girl who answered the phone.

I told her the whole story, how unsure we were about what did happen.

"I'd better come home. Is there going to be a funeral?" her tone started out firm, then wavered into uncertainty. Nell was a good kid in spite of the troubles between us.

"I don't know when it will be. Stay there. You don't want to miss your finals." The combination of grief and uncertainty about Martin's death was overwhelming for me. I didn't want her going through that too.

"I'll skip them. I can make the quarter up."

"No. Just stay. We don't even know what Gwen will decide to do about a funeral."

A silence hung between us on the line. "I guess," she said finally, "but if you think I should come, call and let me know."

"Okay," I said. "Even if it's early?"

She didn't laugh.

Chapter 4

BY THE TIME I left for work that afternoon, I was exhausted but glad to go. Anything to replace the images that occupied my mind: the destruction at Martin's house and Alfred Mallecke, lifeless on a gurney. I splashed water on my face and smoothed my hair back into a barrette. A blue knit skirt with a black sweater fit my mood. Funereal.

The Crisis and Commitment office was quiet after the day shift went home. Cluttered desks jutted from every wall. Out the window, a tiny slice of Puget Sound reflected the city lights. Dirty orange loading cranes lined up in front of the dark sky over Harbor Island like layers of obstacles between me and the reasonable world I'd known yesterday. I usually felt competent at work, but now, I had questions about Alfred Mallecke. I paged through my notes and replayed every word he'd said, but didn't see any other choice I could have made.

Finally, I got a call to come and assess a woman downtown. The location was only a few blocks from the hospital and it took me longer to park the county car than it would have to walk. The city streets were dark and shiny, but Pioneer Square was full of activity. Clubs offered live music and a rotating population of homeless men took up residence on the ornate wrought iron benches in the cobblestone park.

The Star Hotel, just off First Avenue, rented rooms to the indigent of Seattle. Around the corner, business was picking up in the bars. A blues riff drifted from the Central Tavern every time a customer opened the door. I could hear the lyrics, "Ain't superstitious, but a black cat crossed my trail—" The littered sidewalk smelled of urine.

The Star used to be a seaman's hotel known for brawls and transient tenants. Now it housed mainly people struggling with drug addiction or mental illness. It wasn't a very safe place, but for a lot of people, it was home. The evening desk clerk had called for an evaluation of a woman who had been standing in the lobby for a day and a half, yelling back at voices that only she heard.

I spoke into the intercom and waited to be buzzed in. The door had an ornate handle and a beveled glass window. Behind the smudged glass, narrow stairs led to the lobby of the second story hotel. Ten years ago, the first floor had housed a "Live Girls" show. These days, it was boarded up. Renovation for the tourist trade had skipped this block.

The buzzer sounded and I opened the door. In the lobby at the top of the stairs, I saw the woman I was there to assess. She postured, unaware of anyone around her. She was tiny, about thirty-five with light brown hair matted into clumps. She was also about six months pregnant.

"Listen to the underground people. There's poison in the pipes. The gasman burns the children. It's the fires of hell." She spoke in hoarse, rapid spurts and made staccato points with her hands, but her feet didn't move from one spot on the worn linoleum floor.

The room was sepia-toned from the years of nicotine layered on every surface. I threaded my way through the cracked vinyl chairs pulled around the TV. A laugh track blared from the TV and I turned it down as I passed. I recognized the woman. Her name was Liz Larkin. I had evaluated her before.

"Liz, my name is Grace Vaccaro. I'm the county designated mental health professional." We were called MHPs in the vernacular, but I had to say things in an exact way. Otherwise, a very ill person could be released from the hospital on a legal technicality. I explained the legal issues before turning to more personal questions to gain her trust. "I'm here to evaluate you for hospitalization. Do you remember me?"

"Be careful, Grace." She lowered her voice to a secretive level. "The pipes are exploding. I have to pray to make things safe."

Liz had been diagnosed with Schizoaffective Disorder and didn't seem to be taking her medications. She'd had a major breakdown like this a few years ago. At that time, she went to jail after she assaulted passersby in front of Saint James Cathedral. The voices told her to. Assault wasn't okay, but I always liked Liz.

She was in bad shape today—so thin her elbows and collarbones looked sharp in contrast to the roundness of her pregnancy. A dark stain of urine discolored the back of her cotton dress. Her feet may as well have been glued to the floor; Liz wasn't moving far enough to assault anyone at the moment. I was sure I had legal grounds to commit her.

"Can you tell me when you ate last?"

"Pray for the underground people." She swayed back and forth, still rooted to the linoleum. She had on a pair of scuffed brown loafers that were too small for her, the backs mashed down under her bare heels.

"The desk clerk told me that you've been standing here since yesterday morning. Do you remember when you slept last?"

"Slept, kept, leapt. Jack jumped over the candlestick, he's charred and marred, be on your guard. Sleep, slept, slept." Liz didn't look at me as she chanted. She leaned forward from the waist and lost her balance, but she didn't move her feet to catch herself. Before she could topple, I held her shoulders to support the weight until she straightened up. Her off-target responses to my questions made it clear that she couldn't organize her thoughts.

"Are you hearing voices?" I asked.

She nodded and bent her knees for better stability before she leaned forward.

"What do they say?"

"They say, you're going to burn, burn, burn."

"Who's going to burn?"

"I am. The children are. I have to protect the children." She motioned to her feet. "They won't let me go."

I glanced at her belly. That was the child who needed protecting right now. I told her that she would go to the hospital where she'd be safe. I explained the Seventy-Two Hour Hold. Liz nodded. She'd done it all before.

I took a statement from the desk clerk, a skinny old man in a once-white t-shirt, and sat down to write up my affidavit. For legal purposes, her condition was called Grave Disability, meaning she was unable to care for her basic needs like nutrition and rest. An extra concern today was her pregnancy. Liz might be okay, but she could permanently damage her baby. She hadn't even moved to eat or use the bathroom.

To make sure she wasn't held unjustly, Liz would get representation by an attorney and have her case reviewed in court after seventy-two hours. In Washington State, we all knew the story of Frances Farmer. She was from Seattle, a Hollywood actress who was hospitalized by her family for years during the 1940s when her only real problem was a difficult personality. My job was to prevent that from happening again.

The system usually worked, but sometimes families were frustrated when they couldn't get a loved one hospitalized until something terrible happened. At times, the courts released a patient just because the lawyer found a loophole.

Like Liz, I just wanted to protect everybody.

She kept talking and still didn't move her feet when I went over to the desk to arrange for an ambulance to take her to Harborview. I organized the paperwork that would go with her. Legal forms in triplicate covered the scarred reception counter. The clerk watched while I filled them out.

He looked like he'd been there since the old days when the Star rented rooms for fifty cents a night. Gray hair receded to a deep widow's peak over his freckled forehead. His voice was smooth. "I don't mind her ranting in here—if the person they send is as pretty as you."

I didn't take his flirtation too seriously. I'd met a lot of elderly men like him in my job. They didn't know any other way to talk to a woman. I smiled and flashed my wedding ring. "Better not let my husband hear that. He's a jealous man."

"Don't worry, sweetheart. I'll be waiting for you if you ever get tired of him."

I got back to business. He had to make a formal statement about Liz's condition. Next week, he'd be called to testify in court.

I wrote out my part and the clerk chatted. "I've never seen her here before. I could tell she had a place to stay until recently. She was dirty, but didn't look homeless."

She looked homeless now. Her gaunt face made me think of how quickly the vulnerable people of the city could lose their health and safety.

"Doesn't take long, does it, sweetheart?" the clerk said as if he had read my thoughts.

Something about the old man's solicitous tone made me decide to ask about Mallecke. I didn't know if confidentiality laws still applied after death, but I didn't care either. "Did a man named Alfred Mallecke ever stay here?" I described him to the clerk.

"Sounds like a hundred guys I've seen." the clerk said. "Unless . . . Is he the one who always wore that watch cap—a ratty green thing—pulled down to his eyes?"

"Yes."

The clerk was better at descriptions than I was. If I'd been more accurate in describing Martin, the woman at the morgue never would have let me in. "He was killed a few days ago. I'd just evaluated him but didn't detain him. I've been wondering about what happened ever since."

The old clerk leaned his elbows on the reception counter. The scene reminded me of a barroom—like he was ready to slide a whiskey across to the next customer. He had the look of a man who'd seen and heard everything.

"He told me he was getting radio transmissions through his fillings," I said.

"Must be those really old fillings that do that. Cause the people with that transmitter problem always look like they haven't seen a dentist in years." He used the battlefield humor that probably kept him sane, considering what he saw around here every day.

"Who trusts dentists anyway?" I tried to joke back, but I couldn't keep my tone light. "The radio voices told him he was unsafe on the street."

The clerk's look changed from levity to concern. "You're feeling guilty. You can't blame yourself for what happens on the street. A smart lady like you knows that."

I gave him a halfhearted laugh, glad to have been upgraded from beautiful to smart. The clerk wasn't so bad; I could tell he cared about people.

"I need to know what happened. Then I'll decide if I should feel guilty or not. Maybe there was a specific danger and I didn't understand. Maybe he knew something."

The clerk leaned across the counter until he was close enough for me to smell his hair oil. "I'll tell you one thing. Living on the streets is never safe."

The simple truth of his words hung between us. A call on the intercom ended the conversation. The desk clerk reached under a row of dangling keys with yellowed paper tags and pushed a button to open the door on the street.

A young man in converse sneakers climbed the steps two at a time. He was probably in his twenties—Native American with a thick ponytail tied in a rawhide cord. He stopped and spoke to Liz, who didn't respond, then made his way through the maze of chairs to the reception desk. His jeans and t-shirt looked new, and a wool sports jacket was draped in the crook of his arm.

"This lady's here to get help for your friend," the clerk said.

The young man gestured toward Liz and spoke in a soft voice that made me pay attention. "My brother is the baby's father."

Chapter 5

IN SPITE OF THE LOW VOLUME of his voice, the young man carried himself with a casual poise that I'd expect from someone older. "I came down to pick her up, but I couldn't get her to come with me. Now what happens?"

"She'll be in the hospital," I answered. "I can't say more because of confidentiality," I said, knowing I was being selective about upholding it. Liz still postured across the room, intent on her dialogue with the voices. She didn't notice much else, not even her baby's uncle inquiring about the hospitalization.

"Can you tell me this much: If they give her medicine, will it hurt the baby?"

His question was a good one. "The doctors are careful to give medications that have the least effect on a fetus. It's the first trimester when the baby is most vulnerable. Liz is past that. Not eating or taking care of herself would do more harm than medicine at this point."

He looked skeptical.

I went on, "After she gets to Harborview, she could sign a release form so the staff could keep you and your brother informed about her treatment."

The young man considered that and seemed unsure of whether to say more. He frowned and studied a name carved into the old oak counter. "My brother's not in much better shape than she is. Leonard is an alcoholic, recovering most of the time. He has depression too. We just found out that our mother's house was destroyed in that explosion down in Olympia. She was burned pretty badly."

"What explosion?" I asked. I hadn't even listened to the news today.

"Yesterday afternoon, a couple of kids were down by the creek." He leaned on the counter. "They were playing with matches, just kid stuff. Normally the worst that would happen might be to burn down somebody's shed."

"What did happen?"

"A gasoline pipeline goes through the area. There was a leak. The vapor had been collecting for hours. When I saw it on TV, the cloud of smoke looked like Hiroshima. Both boys were killed. My brother took off when he found out about our mother. I'm afraid he's on a binge. I don't know what he'll do when he hears about Liz."

In her way, Liz had been right about the explosions and the fires of hell. It must have looked like that. I wouldn't have changed my determination—that was based on lack of self-care. But people with mental illness usually know what they're talking about.

"I'm sorry about your mother," I said. "Liz has probably been in this shape for a while, though. It could be a relief when she is in the hospital getting help."

"Maybe. They airlifted Mom to the burn center at Harborview. She and Liz will be in the same hospital. How convenient." He said it with an edge of sarcasm, then looked abashed. "Sorry, it's not your fault."

People get angry about involuntary commitment, even when it's needed. No one likes to give up control. I extended my hand. "I'm sorry about your mother and your brother. My name is Grace Vaccaro. Do you mind if I put you down as a contact person? It would help if you tell the hospital about Liz's recent circumstances."

"Richard Black," he took my hand and shook it, and wrote down his phone number. It had a Duvall exchange.

I pointed to the number. "I live out in Duvall too. We must be neighbors."

"I'm staying with my uncle on Big Rock Road. You drive all the way in here every day?"

"Three days a week." I dug around in my purse for my keys. It was getting late. "I'll be heading up to Harborview as soon as the ambulance gets here. Are you going to wait?"

"If you'll be with Liz until they come, I could look around for my brother. There are a few places around here he might have gone." Richard slid one arm into his jacket, but stopped when the ten o'clock news came on. He moved to turn it up. Even Liz listened.

The pipeline explosion was the lead story. They showed clips taken by people on the scene. Richard was right. It did look like Hiroshima. With a huge boom, a mushroom cloud erupted into the sky and moved downstream where the gasoline had flowed into the water. Then, the sky was inky and silent as the water burned. The camera panned to a woody area around the creek bed, now flattened and black. The charred skeleton of a house was next. I looked at Richard.

His expression tightened. "That was my mom's place."

Then, a concerned-looking reporter interviewed the boys' parents who couldn't hold back their tears. The brothers had been airlifted to Seattle, but were dead by evening. Richard's mother was reported as another victim, in stable condition at the Harborview Burn Center.

"Those poor kids," I felt shaken, as if I had been there in the explosion with them. "A gas stove blew up in my face when I was a kid. The flame boomed out like that. But it was nothing compared to what happened to those boys." Unconsciously, I felt for the scar tissue on my left temple, touched by empathy for their pain.

"I hope they didn't feel anything," Richard said. "It happened fast."

"What about your mom?"

"She's going to be okay. She was asleep when it happened so it took her a while to get out. She said it felt like a train hit the house."

On screen, representatives of the Lyster Oil Company offered condolences and denied responsibility. The newscaster said a full investigation of the event was underway, then in typical TV fashion, the story ended in two minutes. Liz went back to posturing in her place behind the chairs and Richard left to find his brother, his own part in mopping up the aftermath of the tragedy.

The buzzer from the street-level door sounded. Two ambulance techs came in and bounced a gurney up the narrow steps. The drivers looked like filling station attendants in navy blue jackets with their company name patch sewn on the front. They joked with the desk clerk, full of jovial good will. I hoped there was an elevator to get them back down.

We converged at the front desk, traded paperwork and went over to Liz. She registered the drivers' presence and slipped one of them right into her delusional system.

"You're the gas man, you brought the poison." Liz held one hand over her head and pointed two fingers at the embroidered name patch he wore. "Stay back."

"Don't worry, ma'am," the closest driver said. He had friendly green eyes that filled with concern when he tried to reassure her. "We're just here to give you a ride to the hospital."

Liz scanned the room, looking for a place to bolt. I had some rapport with her and stepped in with reassurance, but kept an eye on the distance between us because Liz was scared and might become aggressive.

"Don't let him near me. The gas man is the devil."

"Liz, it's okay," I told her. "Remember, you're going to the hospital. It's safe there."

"The devil has green eyes that burn right through me. Keep him away."

And I thought this was going to be easy. Liz had been calm enough when I interviewed her. "He'll stay back. Let me help you get on the gurney."

The ambulance drivers had the narrow stretcher lowered and the blanket folded back, ready for her. Three seat belts dangled from the aluminum frame to fasten her torso and legs. White cloth Posey restraints were tucked underneath and would secure her wrists and ankles during the trip. I was nurturing and cajoling, but she'd have none of it. She knew the ambulance driver would take over as soon as I was done. She held herself rigid and scanned his slightest movement with wild eyes.

People who do this kind of work develop a sixth sense about when they could get assaulted. For me it was a tingling, my instincts preparing to act or get out of the way. The clerk behind the desk held his thumb and pinky out like a telephone receiver and held it to his ear—did I want him to call the police? I gave a quick nod. They were never far away in this neighborhood.

Sweet-talking hadn't worked so I switched to my firm mode. Concrete. "Liz, sit on the gurney. It's better if you do it yourself."

Liz glared. I pointed to the gurney. The desk clerk buzzed the door and two SPD officers started up the stairs. Just having the authorities at hand often did the trick. I didn't think we'd actually have to use the police. I held a finger up for them to wait and they hovered at the top of the steps, assessing the situation.

"I'll have the police stay right there," I told her. "Sit down, please."

Liz weighed the possibilities and sat. The ambulance guys gave her space and she pulled each bony leg onto the gurney with painful slowness. Everybody gave her the time. I kept talking while the drivers secured the straps. Liz exerted every ounce of control she had and let them do it. When she was ready, the clerk showed them to an aged elevator behind the lobby. Before the elevator doors closed, Liz took up her warnings again, telling us about hell and poison, danger from all sides. It seemed like a good description of my day too.

When I got back to the office to finish the never-ending flow of paperwork, a new stack of folders had joined the usual mess in my mail slot. On top of it all was propped a folded piece of paper with my name scribbled on the front in my supervisor's handwriting. I picked off the tape she'd used to seal the note. The prosecutor's office had filed a complaint about the number of people we had detained on inadequate evidence, or what they considered inadequate evidence. It didn't look good when cases didn't hold up in court. According to the note, too many of those cases were mine. Vera wanted to talk.

~

The next morning, I woke up mad. I had the day off, but my thoughts were drawn to the meeting with my supervisor. Vera wanted to talk about hospitalizing fewer people. I'd just done that and a man was dead.

Downstairs, Frank was getting ready for work. I churned in bed until I smelled the coffee, then I went down. I forgot to say good morning and told Frank everything. "The attorneys are afraid they won't look good if they lose too many cases. They're worried about percentages." I sat at the kitchen table with my hair uncombed, teeth unbrushed, and wearing a bathrobe so old that Goodwill wouldn't accept it.

Frank listened while he made breakfast, cracking eggs into the cast iron skillet. A pile of eggshells grew to his right and the smell of browning butter should have made my mouth water.

"Want some?" he asked.

"Just toast." My stomach was already in a knot.

Outside, the sun arced low in the hazy southern sky and wouldn't crest the trees until nine o'clock. Black clouds gathered in the northeast and were already spitting rain across the road.

Frank was dressed for the day in Levi's and an untucked flannel shirt. He turned the eggs, yolks intact, and pushed down the toaster. "What are you going to do?" he asked.

"I want to know what happened to Alfred Mallecke before I talk to Vera on Monday."

Frank prompted me again. "And find out what?"

"Why was he in Duvall? How did he get here?"

Frank brought two plates and tried to get me to eat some eggs anyway. "There's never been a murder out here that I can remember. All of a sudden there are two. Do you think it has something to do with Martin's death?"

I shrugged, feeling helpless. Alfred Mallecke's death was easier for me to talk about. I could deal with being angry; it was the pain of Martin's death I didn't want to face right now.

"The clerk at the Star recognized him. I want to find out if he's seen Mallecke with anyone."

Before Frank could say anything else, I grabbed the phone and called the Star. The clerk I'd talked to was named Odelee Kearn. And I found out that he wasn't scheduled to work again until next Monday. That was when I would meet with Vera. If I wanted to bolster my arguments with facts, it had to happen before then.

I left the dishes in the sink, took a shower and pulled on a pair of jeans. As soon as Frank left for work, I got in my truck and turned toward Seattle. Odelee Kearn was in the phone book. He looked like he might have lived at the Star at one time, but he now had an apartment on Summit Avenue, the flanks of Capitol Hill. His place wasn't much of an improvement.

Capitol Hill sat just above downtown. It was a neighborhood of gracious old homes, vintage apartment buildings and business areas with lively foot traffic. But Summit Avenue was on lower Capitol Hill. Much lower. The crumbling apartment building was sandwiched between a tattoo parlor and a brand new condo.

I hadn't called ahead, but hoped I wasn't making the three-hour round trip for nothing. I wanted to be back in Duvall before rush hour traffic brought the freeways to a standstill.

The front door of the building was propped open with an old phone book. A handwritten slip taped to a row of mailboxes said Odelee Kearn lived in number six. Worn carpet ran down the center of the hallway, with dark wood on either side. The smell of cooked cabbage trapped inside didn't get enough air to dissipate. The old man opened the door when I knocked. He had on the same t-shirt he'd worn last night, or its graying twin, but he was freshly shaven and his receding hair was neatly combed. His age was uncertain, maybe an old-looking sixty-five. Maybe add fifteen.

He concentrated on my face for a minute, like he didn't recognize me out of context. Then he got it. "You finished with that husband of yours so soon?"

"Not quite, this is business. I didn't get a chance to ask you more about Alfred Mallecke."

He invited me in and cleared a pile of newspapers off a kitchen chair. The one room held both his single bed and his kitchen table. There was no other door that would lead to the bathroom. It would be down the hall.

"I don't know how I can help you. Mallecke was the kind of guy who got a room once in a while so he could get out of the weather or get a shower. That's all I know."

"Did you ever see him with anyone? Someone he talked to?"

He shook his head no, but frowned, still thinking. "Well, there is one guy. Bushy beard, long red hair. That's what they call him—Red. He stays under the freeway. Or did. The police go roust them out from time to time. But those guys have to stay somewhere, don't they?"

"How do I get there?" I asked.

We looked at each other. He put his hands out in a gesture that said stop. "Whoa, pretty lady. I stayed down there awhile myself. You don't want to go looking for him there. What do you think you're going to find out, anyway?"

"I won't know until I hear it."

"You're the one who's crazy." He palmed the table to help himself up and pulled a pea coat off the back of the chair. "But I'll take you there. That husband of yours would never forgive me if I let you go by yourself."

33

Chapter 6

FROM DEARBORN STREET we entered a maze of footpaths. Freeway ramps arched to our left and we heard constant waves of tires roaring on the rain-slick pavement. I followed Odelee Kearn down a narrow track carved into shoulder-high blackberry vines with thorns that ripped at my parka. He walked ahead with his head bowed into the steady rain and with his hands stuffed into his coat pockets.

Himalayan blackberries were introduced to the Northwest from India, via England. Like many transplants, no one had guessed how well they would take to the mild, wet climate. Here, the blackberries engulfed any unworked ground in a season; getting rid of them took twenty years. Like the barbed vines that had hidden my rooster from Martin's dog, the blackberries served the same purpose here. The clearing where the homeless lived was concealed from those who didn't already know the way.

I felt like I was entering a no man's land where I didn't know the rules. My skin pricked and I sensed I was being watched.

The camp wasn't actually under the freeway, but next to it, under a couple of tattered lean-tos made from tarps that sagged under the weight of rain pooled in the center. The man we'd come to see sat at the edge of the shelter and warmed his hands over a smoky fire. He lived up to his name with red hair and a beard that bushed out even redder. Layers of coats and sweaters added to a bulky frame. He looked like a medieval warrior and wore an attitude of suspicion like a coat of mail. Even in March, his skin was dark from life outside. Sun and wind and not much soap.

He regarded me with wary eyes. Not paranoid, not delusional, just suspicious. I didn't belong. My escort hung back. It was up to me to do the talking.

I introduced myself. "Mr. Kearn told me you know Alfred Mallecke."

He eyed the old desk clerk but got no response. "I know a lot of people. What's it to you?"

"He was killed."

Smells of human waste and rotten food mingled with the oily freeway fumes. A couple of men seemed to disappear behind the concrete pillars of the ramps. I'd caught glimpses of camps like this before, but only from the road traveling fifty-five miles an hour.

"You're no cop." He got up and picked through a pile of broken-down pallets, chose a splintered piece of wood and tossed it on the fire. "If you were a cop, you'd be walking around here like you had a stick up your ass." His voice was hostile, but maybe he was testing me.

I held my ground. "I'll take that as a compliment."

He barked a single, "Ha," that might have been a laugh, but his cautious squint remained.

I didn't like it here and didn't feel much safer with Odelee Kearn along. He seemed more a tour guide than a bodyguard. I wondered about my own judgment in coming and squared my shoulders to put on a more confident front than I felt. I told Red the truth, that I'd evaluated Mallecke, let him go and wanted to know what happened. "The voices told him he wasn't safe on the street. Was there anything specific he was afraid of?"

"You mean besides hunger, weather, gangs, and cops?"

"Right, besides that." My answer was clipped; his attitude was wearing thin.

"No." Red worked at his teeth with a well-used toothpick and flicked it in the fire. A crust of his most recent meal clung to his beard.

"His body was found out in Duvall. Did he know anyone there?"

"I don't know."

"What about family?"

"Why? You want to adopt him?" His eyes bored into me.

"A little late for that," I said. "Listen, you have no reason to trust me. But what harm will it do? Mallecke's dead. If he has family, I can notify them. I want to know if his death could have been prevented."

Red laughed. "Lady, look around you. Do you think you can prevent anything that happens in a world like this? You're not that big."

The gray sky blended into the concrete and the underbrush wore a dismal coating of grit. The other men from the camp stayed just out of view in the dimmer shadows of the overpass.

Red kicked at the fire with his boot and a rush of sparks and ash flew up. "Get out of here," he said. "Mallecke wasn't like me. He was always helping people. Last time I saw him he was helping some bitch, crazier than he was. He thought he could help. That's not a mistake I plan to make with you."

He lunged in my direction and threw his arms forward like he was going to grab, or maybe shove, me. I jumped away and then hated myself for letting him see that he had intimidated me. But he had. Every cell in my body went on alert.

"Fine, let's go," I said and turned to Odelee, but not so fast that I would show more fear. Odelee, who hadn't said a word, led the way back through the tangled path. I felt Red's stare burn into me, but I didn't look back.

~

My foot itched on the gas pedal. I would have gone seventy to make it home before rush hour, but the traffic had clotted already. Lines of cars stretched across both spans of the I-90 bridge and disappeared into the wet blur of road and lake and sky.

The link between Mallecke and Martin nagged at me. Alfred was homeless but tried to help people. He had rough friends. His body was found close to Martin's.

With Martin, I knew more but had more questions. Someone had rifled Martin's film equipment and stolen his computer; Martin had a box of human bones in his shed. I saw no connection with Mallecke.

The sky spat cold rain and my tires hissed on the road. I was no wiser when I rounded the final bend before my house. A car backing out of Martin's driveway blocked my lane. I slammed on the brakes.

The driver left her silver Mazda half-blocking the road, got out and marched around to talk to me. It was a county council member I was acquainted with. I glanced in my mirror; we didn't have a lot of traffic here but enough to make me worry about getting rear-ended. I rolled down my window.

She extended her hand into the Toyota to shake mine. "You remember me. Lydia Taylor." She was about forty and was dressed for a business meeting, not a day in the country. Her stylish dark hair flattened fast in the rain.

"I'm going to move my truck," I said and shifted into reverse. She was forced to withdraw her hand. I parked in a gravel turnaround across the road. She got the idea and moved her Mazda back into Martin's driveway.

What I remembered about Lydia was her finely honed sense of self-importance. She was the kind of person who expected traffic to stop for her. But her raincoat and pumps were spattered with mud and I felt chastened. Maybe she was in trouble.

I pulled up the hood on my parka and met her in Martin's driveway. "Are you all right?"

"I need to get some things out of Martin's house." No preamble about his death. I wondered if she knew.

"I'm sorry, maybe you haven't heard. Martin was . . . he died."

"Of course I heard. That's why I need to get these papers. We were working on a project together, a community theater proposal."

"I don't know if that's okay," I said. "His sister will be in charge of the estate, but she's very upset. His death has been hard on us all, to tell you the truth."

A light mist drizzled down on us as if a cloud had descended. Heavier drops of water splattered from the trees that lined the driveway. I expected Lydia to soften, but she barely blinked. "This was very important to him. I doubt anyone else would be able to recognize the papers. I'll need to go in—but the house is locked."

"Someone ransacked—"

Lydia cut me off. "I was working with him on a film for the historical society. I need it before the county council meeting this evening."

She must have misinterpreted the dumbstruck look on my face. "There's a public hearing at the community center. A rock quarry is proposed near here."

"I know about the meeting." The quarry was controversial. The meeting would probably be packed, but it was the last thing on my mind with all that had happened. "Martin gave me a copy of the film."

"You have it?"

"Sure, I could make a copy for you. But you'll have to talk to Gwen about the papers."

"I need that film now, so I can review it before the meeting."

I suddenly felt very protective of it. Lydia's sense of entitlement rankled me—and her interest in the disc made me more curious about the break-in at Martin's house. "I haven't had a chance to watch it myself. You'll have to wait."

"It was commissioned and paid for by the historical society. It does not belong to you."

"Lydia, what's the matter with you? Don't you care about anything but your projects? Martin is dead. Nothing is that important right now, except paying him respects."

She held her stomach as if I'd hit her. Confusion, then sadness crossed her face. "You think I don't know that. You have no idea." Her voice dropped.

"You have no idea how I feel," she repeated. "This is what Martin wanted. I need the film now."

I never responded well to bullying. "Have the historical society contact me if you want a copy." I turned my back on her, crossed the road, got in my truck and pulled away.

Lydia's car door slammed and gravel crunched under her tires. From my rearview mirror, I saw her spin out of the driveway and back across the road—in front of an oversize Ford truck that was barreling around the blind curve. The Ford skidded but stopped in time. Lydia straightened out her car and drove away without so much as a wave to the driver.

I pulled up to my house and rested my head on the steering wheel before I turned off the engine. I wondered if Lydia had tried to walk into Martin's house and take whatever she wanted. She had expected the house to be unlocked.

Chapter 7

I FUMBLED WITH MY HOUSE KEYS on the front stoop. The weather report predicted a late snow in the foothills and I tasted the front moving in. Definitely colder than the usual rainy and forty-five degrees. A few tentative flakes of snow began to fall.

The house was dark. My grandfather originally bought the one room cabin in the thirties. He added on every few years until it rambled down to the pond with the rooms lined up shotgun style. The end result was low and wide and clad in rough-cut cedar boards. Casement windows and a French door ran along the front. Frank and I took over the place after my grandparents died. Inside, it was a hodge-podge of my grandmother's old furniture and the touches that we added.

All I wanted was another shower, to scrub off the grime I'd carried with me from the freeway encampment. My encounter with Lydia Taylor didn't help. She left me feeling sullied in a different way. I stripped off my clothes and let them lay where they fell. Under the spray, I scrubbed and let the needles of hot water pummel my skin, but no matter how long I let the water stream over me, something deeper couldn't be cleaned.

Frank would be home soon, covered with a layer of more wholesome dirt from his work. He'd been the first in his family to go to college but later followed his father into the family carpentry business anyway. Sometimes I wished I had a trade like that, where I could step back and see a finished product, something solid and substantial, instead of another troubled person safe in the hospital but just for now.

After the shower, I looked for something to wear, but the damp jeans I'd left on the floor had been the last clean pair. I paced the bedroom in nothing but a chenille sweater and panties until goose bumps raised on my legs. I finally found a pair of worn-out cords with shiny knees and pulled them on.

When I heard Frank pull up, I ran down to meet him. He saw my agitation and held me. The smell of freshly cut lumber clung to his clothes and hair. Then he went to get us both a beer from the refrigerator. "What did you find out?"

I told him about my trip to the freeway camp, but Odelee Kearn had been right on target when he joked about my husband's attitude about the trip to visit Red. Frank worked the bottle opener harder than needed. "You're taking this too far, Grace. Going to a place like that."

"I was looking for information about Mallecke. We discussed it this morning. After that note from Vera at work, I wanted—"

"I didn't mean for you to walk into a dangerous situation."

"Quit being paternal. I don't need your approval to go there. Besides, nothing happened." I took a sip of the beer. "Listen, there's something else. On my way home, I ran into—almost literally—Lydia Taylor backing out of Martin's driveway."

"County council?"

"Yeah. She came out for the quarry meeting tonight and was very insistent about getting things from Martin's house—the film in particular. She demanded that I give it to her."

"You must have liked that. About as much as my suggestion that you consider my feelings when you put yourself in danger." One corner of his mouth went up in an ironic smile. Frank pulled the rocking chair over by the fire.

"Lydia was too demanding about getting into Martin's house. I don't think her reasons about the film or the community theater explained it. I want to go to the quarry meeting to see what she's up to."

"None of this is going to bring Martin back, any more than rooting around under the freeway will bring your Alfred Mallecke back."

"He's not my Alfred Mallecke. I wish you'd come to the meeting with me."

He sat back and folded his arms in front of him. "I guess I deal with things differently. Tonight's poker at Steve's."

I stared at him in disbelief. "You're going to poker after all this?"

"What I want to do is blow off steam. You should too. Call Gwen or something. I'm as upset as you are."

But I didn't think he was. We'd both lost Martin, but I'd also lost Mallecke and my confidence in my work. Frank spent the day doing carpentry; if his corners weren't square, he'd shim them, or start over. I couldn't start over with Alfred Mallecke.

"You should come to the meeting tonight." Maybe I meant to say I needed him, but I didn't. We were squaring off.

"It won't change anything, Grace. Why can't you let it go?"

"You let too much go."

Frank didn't respond. He got up and shuffled through a pile of CDs on top of the stereo, pulled one out and examined it for dust. He slid it into the tray on the player and started it up, a cello concerto that sounded like a dirge.

"No wonder you're getting so involved with the murders, you have to control everything," he said. "You do it all the time. Like with Nell. When I talked to her, she said she'd wanted to come home. But you told her not to."

"What's Nell got to do with this? She's a kid. There's no reason for her to go through all the uncertainty around Martin's death."

"She's not a kid any more. You can't protect her from her own feelings. You try to control her too much. You can't fix everything."

"Oh, I see where this is going, another useful commentary on Grace, the control freak—time to bring that up. We haven't had this argument in almost a month."

Frank turned the volume of the music low and leaned forward. "Nell could deal with Martin's death like the rest of us, maybe better. But not when Grace is in charge."

"Just stop." I escaped to the kitchen and ran a glass of water from the tap. I let the cold water spill over my hands.

"Don't walk away." Frank followed me and turned off the faucet to get my attention. "Maybe you wished your mother gave you more direction. She left you to flounder, but believe me, you've over-compensated."

I turned the glass over, poured the water back into the sink and set it down empty. "You don't have to bring my mother into this. You know that's a sore spot."

A rational part of my brain said that we had both over-reacted because of the murders. But there was a kernel of truth in what Frank said about Nell and my mother. He just had very bad timing in discussing it.

~

Gwen had taken the whole week off from her teaching job to settle Martin's affairs and make arrangements for a memorial on Sunday. When I called, she said she'd tried to spend the morning sorting through his house and papers by herself but had given up, overwhelmed. She was ready for company. We agreed to meet at the community center.

The public commentary was already underway when I elbowed my way through the crowded room and found an open spot to stand by the wall. All the seats were taken. Local residents sprawled in uneven rows of folding chairs and repre-sented all the stages of the valley's history. Old guard loggers, aging hippies and the high tech crowd all sat side by side with members of the Snoqualmie Tribe. I was surprised to see Richard Black, the young man I'd met at the Star Hotel. He looked earnest; he wore a button-down collared shirt under the wool suit jacket this time.

The quarry proposal had stirred up a lot of animosity. The rocky west slope of the Cascades already suffered from mining—

and the big double-axle trucks full of stone that rumbled through town. Duvall was squeezed by suburban sprawl on the west and projects like the Cascade Rock Company's quarry on the east. The quarry would be a violent rending of the beautiful hillside at Cathedral Falls. It seemed to represent everything that had happened, murders and the loss of trust in the small town.

Fluorescent lights cast a pallid light on the crowd. By my count, a hundred people sat in the room. I looked around and saw the usual faces—the same people who turned out for PTA and community fundraisers. I didn't want a quarry, but I hadn't been active in opposing it. Martin had.

Lydia Taylor was the moderator. She'd dried her hair and wiped her shoes since I'd seen her. Even in her business clothes she had the look of someone who had grown too tall too soon and never been comfortable in her body. But she was in her sphere tonight and surveyed the room as if it were a kingdom to be conquered. People from the audience took turns standing to speak.

An older man next to Richard Black rose. "My name is Felix George. I'm a member of the Snoqualmie Tribe. With development moving further east from Seattle, our village and gravesites have been lost to road construction, dams and other so-called progress." He was a barrel-chested man, with white brush-cut hair. His voice was serious, but he spoke with a lilt at the end of each sentence, a storytelling cadence. He got my attention when he spoke of graves. I wondered about the bones in Martin's shed.

"Our ancestors have lived in the valley for 8,000 years. When whites first arrived, the tribe had fourteen villages up and down the river. Three or four thousand people lived in long houses during the winter and moved to camps in the mountains for the summer. Now our number is a tenth of that."

Lydia sat at a long table that faced the rest of the room. She extended her hand, palm out to interrupt his flow. "Thank you, Mr. George, but please restrict your comments to the quarry."

"Cathedral Falls is a sacred place to our people." He got back to the topic, but his voice lost its warmth. "The Cascade Rock Company's plan would destroy it. This gravel pit is like all the other development out here. You want me coming into your Forrest Grove Cemetery and saying, 'Who cares about these old bones? Let's build right over them because I can make some money here.' You can call it progress if you want. I call it desecration."

Lydia leaned forward in her seat at the table. "You're saying that Cathedral Falls is a burial site for your people? Where?"

"I don't give locations."

"I see." Lydia made a note on a legal pad in front of her and then rolled the pen between her palms. She gazed at Felix George and affected a look of compassion. "Your argument would be more compelling if you identified the place. The Council can't act on—"

Felix George bristled and Richard Black put a restraining hand on the older man's arm. He didn't calm much; his words were bitter. "I'll give you compelling. The Native American Graves Protection and Repatriation Act was created to protect our gravesites. The federal government will stop work there until an archaeologist has examined the property. The Cascade Rock Company better be prepared to comply. I can have them shut down."

Chapter 8

THE CROWD REACTED to Felix George's certainty. Chairs scraped, and the audience craned their necks to get a better view. An undercurrent of comments made the speakers hard to hear. The door opened at the back of the room, and Gwen entered with a flash of reds, pinks and oranges from her flowing skirt. She inched past people standing at the back to join me. I put my arm around her in greeting, relieved that she looked a little better. I filled her in on what had happened in the meeting.

"You know Felix George?" she said. "He's one of the elders Martin filmed for the historical society up at Cathedral Falls."

"He's talking about grave sites being up there. Do you think he knew about the bones in Martin's shed?"

Gwen's expression tightened at the question, but she shook her head. "I don't know. Do you think he can actually stop the quarry?"

I held a finger up for Gwen to wait. Lydia had changed the direction of the meeting. I wanted to hear.

She introduced the men promoting the gravel pit. The Cascade Rock Company wasn't a big business from out of town that people railed against on principle. It was a local family enterprise. Lewis Swan, the patriarch, had made a small fortune buying and selling property. His son, Bob, was an aging relic of the counter culture and a fixture in town.

Bob made his way to a makeshift podium set on a long cafeteria table. His blond hair was shaggy in that once-every-six-months haircut some men out here favored. He gripped the stand and looked out at the roomful of neighbors who disagreed with him. His voice was thin. "We're here to listen to your concerns and work with you to make the quarry safe. I've hired a soils engineer to make recommendations about where to cut for minimum damage to the environment..."

Bob moved his eyes around the room as if he'd just studied a book on public speaking. When he made eye contact with Felix George, an electric charge seemed to bind the men's stares. The look Felix George pinned him with was more than suspicious, it was like Felix could see right into him and read the omissions in Bob's speech, the damage to the aquifer, the destruction of sacred ground and maybe each sin Bob had ever committed. The stare shut Bob down. He fumbled with his baseball cap, turning it over in his hands, a permanent indentation of crimped hair marked its place on his head.

"I hear the quarry was Bob's brain child," I whispered to Gwen.

She snorted. "Bob was in my French class back in the seventies and if his brain ever had children, I couldn't tell. He's not up to this crowd."

Lewis Swan nudged his son away from the stand, ready to do damage control. He tried to mollify us with saccharine words. "I understand your apprehension about the quarry. Our family has lived in Duvall since 1917. I was born on Virginia Street in 1921. There was a gravel pit on the banks of the Snoqualmie River then, right behind town. I took a walk there yesterday, a very rainy walk, I admit."

People chuckled, but it was grudging.

"I was looking for it and I really couldn't tell where that gravel pit had been," he continued.

Both of the Swan men had thin, concave bodies. On Lewis, the posture seemed predatory. He was a businessman from way back. He gestured comfortably, reaching out to the crowd. His thinning hair was combed straight back and emphasized the hawk-like effect of his narrow face. "Of course the quarry will have an impact. It will change an area that is beautifully wooded

47

today. It too will regenerate. We promise to leave a buffer of trees to screen it from view. But an effect we haven't mentioned tonight is jobs. Up to one hundred local jobs will be created by this quarry. One hundred needed jobs . . . "

"Maybe his son could get one. He needs a job." Gwen whispered and raised one eyebrow.

"He does pick-up work," I said. "You know, Martin was one of the people he did jobs for."

"Oh, I know. Martin was all worked up last week, trying to reach Bob. I didn't think anything of it at the time. But now I wonder if it was about more than an odd job."

Bob looked more like the hired help up front with Lydia and his father. He wore the ubiquitous plaid shirt and jeans in a faded, baggy-in-the-butt version and a hat advertising Stihl chain saws. He shuffled it from hand to hand.

It was the elder Swan that infuriated me. I raised my hand and Lydia pointed in my direction.

"This was a sparsely populated part of the state in 1921. The environmental impact statement mentions ground water contamination, and my well is just down stream." The anger in my voice surprised me. Outside, a storm had blown in. A gust of wind spattered the community center windows with freezing rain. Electric heaters along the walls cranked out too much heat. The air was dank with the wet-animal smell of wool; people peeled off extra sweaters.

Lewis Swan regarded me seriously. "The quarry will meet all federal standards for run-off. But you should have city water soon."

I'd been a silent objector on the quarry issue until now, but Cathedral Falls held a special significance for me. I remembered picnics at the foot of the falls on sticky summer days, making sandwiches with my grandmother, laughing when icy spray from the water crashing to the rocks soaked us. My grandparents had homesteaded in the Snoqualmie Valley. When I was growing up, I spent all my summers with them. It was a world apart from life in the city with my mother. She couldn't help it, but Frank was right—she had left me to flounder. There were too many times when she went to bed in the middle of the afternoon and her depression kept her there for days.

"We'll have city water and a polluted creek." A neighbor from two properties down seconded my argument.

But I wasn't done yet, I'd done some reading before I came. "The mining contractor you're using breached the aquifer ten miles south of here. Every well in that area went dry. People can't afford the thousands of dollars it costs to hook up to city water."

"The federal government has strict guidelines. We will follow those to the letter." Lewis Swan was terse when people didn't agree with him, but his smile didn't slip.

The opposition continued for an hour, until Lydia Taylor cut it off and promised to take it under consideration, which meant disregard it, as far as I could tell.

"Or maybe we'll see you in court," I mouthed in Mr. Swan's direction.

Gwen and I wove our way to the front of the community center. Men and women milled in the aisles between the folding chairs and pulled on coats. The room was a study in greens and browns. People in the Northwest dressed to match the landscape outside—except for Gwen, who provided a bright spot in a sea of dreariness.

In a town of a few thousand people, news of Martin's death had spread fast. Gwen was overwhelmed by a surge of hugs from people who wanted to offer condolences for her brother. I bumped through the crowd behind her, listening to the theories and misinformation that had spread in just one day. Questions about the murder, but no certainty.

Lydia approached me and clutched my arm. I pulled back a little. With her height, I thought it was intimidation, but her manner had changed since our afternoon encounter. "I'm sorry if there are any bad feelings after this afternoon, Grace. I'm not dealing with Martin's death very well either."

A navy blue thread had come loose from a buttonhole on her jacket. Lydia wrapped and unwrapped it around a manicured nail.

"That's okay," I said, unsure if Lydia was sincere.

"Martin and I worked so hard on those projects. Going forward with them was, in my mind, a way to pay respects. I get too focused sometimes. We were talking to the historical society about turning that old farm house they have into a theater," Lydia said. "But they wanted it for a museum."

Martin had been interested in a theater, I knew that. He was always wheeling and dealing for some community improvement or other. But he'd never mentioned Lydia Taylor.

"We had plans drawn up. Martin . . . " She stopped when she said his name and looked confused. She still held on to me, her fingers wrapped around my forearm as if I were an anchor. "It doesn't matter now. The whole idea seems trivial."

I believed her now. She was taking it hard and even though I didn't like Lydia, I put my hand over hers and steered her toward the door. The room felt too confining.

Outside, the night was wintry. We stepped away from the entrance and stood under the wide eaves. The community center was nestled at the edge of a dark stand of Douglas fir. The trees rocked in the wind and pelted us with half-frozen drops of water. The fabric of Lydia's suit coat wicked the dark wet spots into a larger stain.

Lydia looked toward the parking lot and seemed startled. "Oh, my husband's here." She motioned toward a tall man standing beside a new Land Cruiser double-parked in the small lot.

From a distance, he looked like what a young Tom Hanks would look like if he were a little more handsome. I could picture him in an advertisement with the wet road and the highly waxed SUV reflecting lights on a black night. He scanned the crowd, spotted Lydia and walked over.

"What are you doing here?" she said in a hushed voice. "I told you I wouldn't need a ride." She leaned toward him as if she'd forgotten me.

"I just thought I'd see how the meeting went, maybe meet you in town for a bite to eat." He smiled at her in a way that seemed romantic and I wondered how long they'd been married.

Lydia turned back. "Oh, excuse me. This is Grace Vaccaro." She waved a hand between us. "My husband, Will Taylor."

He put one hand out to shake mine, at the same time he draped an arm around Lydia's shoulder. "Got all the community complaints done?"

"I wouldn't say the community is finished." I bristled at his assumption that our comments were nothing more than an inconvenience before the bulldozers came. "We blocked another quarry on Novelty Hill Road."

"Sorry. I didn't mean to offend. It's just that Lydia's put so much into this project." He gave her shoulder a proprietary squeeze. "What people don't understand is how much their services will improve if you get a bigger tax base out here. Are you a local business owner?"

"No, I work in Seattle—in mental health."

"Now for commuters, it's good . . . Mental health, that's interesting. What do you do?"

"I evaluate people for involuntary commitment."

Lydia's husband let out a low whistle. "I'll watch what I say around you. You might send me away—where? You send people to the state hospital?"

"Sometimes," I answered. I got this reaction from strangers often enough, especially when they were uncomfortable with people who seemed different.

"I've always wondered about that. Well, I wouldn't want you to send me there."

I looked back toward the community center, not wanting to miss Gwen.

"Will," Lydia leaned close to whisper in her husband's ear, "maybe you could satisfy your interest in mental health some other time. Your car is blocking the exit."

He glanced over his shoulder, where meeting-goers trying to leave the parking lot were shooting him dirty looks. Lydia and her husband were a good match, same misguided boosterism, same sense of entitlement.

"Right. Better go. Let's meet in town for pizza. That's probably all you can get out here until you beef up the tax base." He smiled in my direction, seemingly pleased to have gotten in the last word on local issues, and said good-bye.

Lydia gave him a kiss. "Nice talking with you, Grace. By the way, I'd still love to have a copy of those films. Whenever you can get around to it."

Chapter 9

WARMLY LIT WINDOWS greeted me when I rounded the last curve before home. I was drawn to the light but disappointed when I got there. Inside, the rooms were quiet. Frank wasn't back yet from his night out; he'd just left the lamps on. I tossed a log into the wood stove and waited for it to kindle with the leftover coals. I hoped our argument didn't reignite too. Frank and I could never talk our way out of arguments. We only progressed to meaner and more hurtful jabs.

Lydia's remark about Martin's film spurred my curiosity. Until now, I had avoided watching it, afraid the reminder of him would be too painful. So I braced myself for the onslaught of feelings, made a cup of tea and found the disc in the pile of books and mail on my desk. We kept the television in the tiny cabin by the pond. Nell took the TV with her when she claimed the little guest house as her own. I grabbed my coat for the walk fifty feet through the garden. Outside, the rain had changed to fat, wet flakes of snow that quickly covered the ground where only the skeletons of weeds pushed through. My feet left a wet trail on the stone path between the houses.

Nell's space felt lonely; my distance from her, and now from Frank, was like a specter in the unheated rooms. Spiders had taken up residence in the corners. I cranked the electric heater to high and the cobwebs shivered in the updraft.

I dropped the disc into the DVD player and heard a tapping from outside. Frank pushed the door open a crack and stuck his head in. He waited there, half in, as if he were afraid to come farther. "Are we still fighting?"

"No," I said, although I was reserving judgment until I saw what kind of mood he was in. "I didn't expect you home so soon."

Frank pushed his hands deep into the pockets of his jacket. Snowflakes clung to his hair. "I ducked out early. Is that the historical society movie?"

"Yeah. You win anything?"

"I broke even. It's bad form to leave if you're winning. Everybody wants to make his money back." He sounded a little loose. Frank sat down on the far end of the couch like we were a couple on a first date. Even from here, I could smell the bourbon and cigar smoke. He pulled off his boots and kicked them to the floor with two hollow thunks, then propped his feet on the ottoman.

Neither of us spoke for a minute, then Frank cleared his throat. "What I said earlier, about your mother and Nell. I overstated that." He touched my shoulder.

I didn't soften. What I really wanted to hear was "I'm sorry. I love you."

"Your mother had no business being a parent, or a single parent anyway. I hate to see you make the opposite mistake with Nell, though."

"What do you want me to do? Call Nell back and tell her to come home? She'll lose the whole semester of credits."

Frank thought a moment. "Gwen's set the date for the memorial. Let Nell decide, instead of being so quick with an answer."

"I'll call in the morning."

He slid over and wrapped his arms around me. "Don't worry so much. She'll do fine."

I gave him a stiff-backed hug and handed him the remote control. "I don't want to fight—I'm just in a terrible mood. Let's watch."

Frank pressed the remote to begin the film. After the opening credits were finished, it became clear that Martin had used the river as the film's centerpiece. The opening frames showed yellowed photographs, a log boom moving downstream to Everett, an early 1900s swimming party, complete with girls in bloomers.

The pictures lulled me into a safer time. The cycles of the seasons reeled by. Summer, when the water dropped and left a sandy beach. Autumn, when the fall rains came in earnest, the river muddied and swelled and left the banks at flood stage. Salmon followed the water back into the streams and fought the strong currents to spawn and die. Some years fall's temperatures were warm enough to melt early snow in the mountains and runoff added to the rain-heavy load that already filled the river.

The big floods were never forgotten. November of 1990 brought the largest flood in local memory. Families moved to the upper floors of their houses to stay dry. They ferried provisions in by boat and passed boxes of food and bottled water through bedroom windows. That year, all access to the west was cut off for days, the main bridge undermined by persistent currents.

I changed my position on the couch; I was uncomfortable. Martin was found dead at the river. The surface of floodwater looked still and quiet. An old man in overalls told stories of people who underestimated its power, drove through flooded roads, and were stranded when their engines stalled. The lucky spent the night in a tree and waited for the flood to crest.

Then the film moved to the hills. "There's Cathedral Falls," Frank waved the remote and hit the pause button, leaving the torrent of water suspended on the screen.

Martin had used the falls Bob Swan wanted to quarry as an example of the environment before the influence of settlers. The narrow stream rushed over the shoulder of an escarpment and fell to the mossy rocks below. A single yellow leaf drifted down to the water. Sunlight dappled the forest floor where the stems of wild geraniums had gone red. Tribal members spoke of sacred places.

"That's Felix George," I said, "from the quarry meeting."

He spoke in that same storytelling voice, as he handled stone artifacts unearthed by Seattle's water department when they built their new treatment plant a few miles down the road. The narrator talked about the history of the area's first inhabitants, how they had made permanent settlements with longhouses built of cedar. Then the film blurred back to forest and ended with Native American music, a lone drum and mournful voice.

"You could use this for the memorial," Frank said.

"I guess I'd hoped the film would answer some questions about the murders." I reached for the remote and played the section with the falls and Felix George over again as if it held some answer that I could almost see in the swirling leaves that touched the water. "Martin and Alfred Mallecke were found at the river. And Cathedral Falls will be destroyed. Could Martin have come across something while he was filming?" I asked and wondered what to do next.

Frank lowered his head a notch and pinched the bridge of his nose. It looked like he was concentrating, but it was probably a headache creeping in as the alcohol wore off. "I don't know."

I pushed rewind and watched the images speed backward on the screen.

~

The next morning continued dark and cold, but five inches of snow covered the ground and made the world look clean. Frank and I set our disagreements aside and lingered at the kitchen table with the newspaper. He monopolized the front section and read an article on the oil pipeline out loud. The explosion was big news.

"The pipeline is owned by a company called Lyster. Their last inspection showed hundreds of defects. Three were in the section of pipe that ruptured in Olympia last week. Lyster didn't find them important enough to repair at the time."

"Isn't that the same company that wants to put a new pipeline through Fall City?"

"Oh yeah, ten miles from here. They withdrew the application for the Cascade pipeline right after the explosion. They're going to resubmit after they finish investigating the accident in Olympia."

I cleared away the dishes and filled the sink with soapy water. "I heard that two hours before the explosion, an alarm went off at Lyster alerting them to a problem with that pipe. They turned off the alarm and went about business as usual."

"The Swan's gravel pit doesn't sound so bad in comparison." Frank stood up and made a neat pile of the newspaper, then joined me at the sink. He wrapped his arms around me and stopped the dishwashing project. "I'm sorry about last night."

I leaned into him. "I'm sorry too."

He pulled my shirt off my shoulder and grazed my skin with a kiss. His breath was warm. "When we first moved here, I thought we'd found paradise. It was like stepping back in time."

"I still love it when I drive across the valley and see the hills behind town." I moved his hands down from the hollow of my collarbone and then pressed against him. We both needed to get away from the realities of the past week, even if it was just for a little while.

"There's a big encroachment on paradise these days," Frank said.

Out the window, snow laced the bare branches of the alders. Martin's roof showed white beyond the trees, a sad reminder of the empty house. I shifted my weight and turned. "Let's go upstairs and try to forget." I stepped back and pulled the plug on the dishwater in the sink. It drained away.

We started toward the stairs, but the phone rang.

"Maybe it's Nell." I found the portable phone under the stack of newspapers and grabbed it just before the answering machine picked up. It clicked dead as soon as I said hello.

"Who is it?" Frank asked.

"A hang up call." I tossed the phone onto the desk and followed him upstairs.

Chapter 10

BY AFTERNOON, life seemed brighter. Frank and I parted with a kiss on the front porch and left on separate errands. A few tired flakes still fell from the sky and dirty ridges of snow lined the road where it had been plowed and sanded. By the time I reached the valley, it seemed to be another season altogether. Horses, heavy and ready to foal, grazed the green fields. At the bottom of Cherry Valley Road I turned left into town.

I had called Gwen before I left the house and promised to help her plan the memorial and make copies of Martin's film. We agreed to show it—a poignant reminder of his place in the community. Afterward, the copies sat on the truck seat beside me like they were charged with a life of their own. Maybe someone else could find something Frank and I missed—something about what happened to Martin. I planned to give one to the police, the rest to everyone else I could think of, even Lydia.

There was still enough time before dark to take a walk by the river after I left Gwen's. Part of me hoped the exercise would clear my head. But I had other reasons. Railroad tracks had once paralleled the water. Now, the grade was paved for a walking trail. I turned north, pulled by a morbid desire to see the place where Martin and Alfred Mallecke had been found. The river reflected the flat gray of the sky. I hadn't walked far when I found the yellow crime scene tape flapping in the breeze. It still blocked the trail and cordoned off a steep hillside at the river's edge. I stepped over. Inside the circle, the air felt heavier.

I hurried out of the marked area and walked faster to leave the feeling behind. In a marshy depression on the other side of the path, redwing blackbirds raised a menacing chatter. Half a mile farther, a skinny dog nosed at a ripped plastic garbage bag and ran when I came near.

The mess was one more symbol of destruction. I squatted to clean it up and carry the trash back to a garbage can in town, a small act that couldn't begin to restore the order in our lives. I picked up the sticky mess with two fingers. Individual packets of sugar, salt and pepper were stuck together from the wet. The dog left a ripped pile of cereal boxes. Crumbs coated a pile of folded clothing.

I had seen this before, the belongings of a homeless person. The single serving foods were easy to carry and wouldn't spoil. The clothes had been stacked neatly, but reeked of cigarettes and dirty feet. Instead of hastily piling the contents back into the bag, I picked up each item with reverence, believing it had belonged to Alfred Mallecke. He might have stashed his things in a hiding place that the police hadn't found, far from the cordoned area.

Under the clothing, I found a stack of papers, soft and frayed at the corners from being carried and rearranged so long. Appointment slips bore Mallecke's name. My hands shook with excitement at the proof that the bag was really his. Bottles of psychiatric medications, empty, lay underneath. It looked like he'd run out months ago.

I dug to the bottom and found a tiny plastic statue of the Virgin Mary, with a broken hand. I cradled it and wiped away a smudge of dirt, then I tucked it into my coat pocket. It wasn't important to the police and wouldn't help the investigation. I wanted something to remember him by. Then I hurried back to the truck and took both the bag and Martin's film to the police station with instructions for the receptionist to give them to Carl Ring.

The roads turned snowy again on the gentle climb out of the valley. A canopy of evergreens absorbed the last light of the day. When my house came into view, I looked for the windows across the back to be lit, for Frank to be home with the fire going, but everything was dark.

I picked up an armful of firewood on my way in. With the logs balanced on my hip, I swung the door open. The air felt too cold. Cold like it had been empty for days. I dumped the wood on the porch and rushed around the corner to the kitchen. In the moment it took to get there, I knew how foolish I was to go in.

The back door hung broken and splintered. I scanned the dark corners of the kitchen. There was no broken door at Martin's. But we kept ours locked; our door was kicked in. Jagged glass pointed from the top half of the Dutch door like barbs. The frame peeled away from the wall and the wood hung in slivers where it split. Snow drifted in from the deck.

I stepped over the broken glass and examined the wreckage. Strange thoughts enter my mind at times like that. I thought about how I had just washed that window and the effort was wasted. I didn't think about how the person who had done it might still be around. At least I didn't think about it right away.

Chapter 11

A CRASH AND THE SOUND OF BREAKING GLASS ended my reverie. The echo reverberated in the circle of trees around the house and could only have come from Nell's cabin fifty feet from where I stood. I jumped back to the illusion of safety in the house.

"Frank! Get the gun. There's someone in the little house," I screamed in a wild bluff that I hoped would scare the intruder off. I was more the gun control type and Frank was nowhere in sight.

I hesitated, poised in the back door, ready to run out through the front. But I wanted to know what I was running from and tried to see through the screen of bamboo that lined the garden between the houses.

Lights from the cabin threw inky shadows into the clearing. After the initial crash, the only sound was the rattle of dry bamboo in the wind. My muscles ached from tension. Then I thought of Dave Bender, our neighbor across the road. He littered his yard with NRA signs at election time. Smith and Wesson bumper stickers covered the back of his truck. I'd go there. I was willing to be flexible in my "no gun" ideology given the circumstances.

The back door to the cabin banged open before I could run. A dark shape that looked like a slender man paused. The back deck jutted over the pond and the only exit was through a leafless tangle of salmonberries and alder. He turned toward the woods but slipped with a splash and a gasp. He landed in the pond. I heard the sucking sound of water breaking when he climbed out. Branches snapped. He pushed through the underbrush.

That was when I broke for Dave and the Smith and Wesson. I half ran, half slid down the driveway. Dave's lights came into view across the road and I thanked God he was home. I pounded on the door and barged in before he could answer. "Call the police. Someone broke into my place. He's still there."

Dave looked up from the circle of light cast by a floor lamp next to his easy chair. His stringy build and loose-fitting work clothes made me feel like I'd run into a scene from a Norman Rockwell painting. It felt like an hour, but was probably seconds, before Dave threw down the newspaper and grabbed the phone. He dialed first and asked questions later.

Dave spoke quickly to the dispatcher and slammed down the phone. "Do you think he's still there?"

"He was running in the woods when I left." I said, breathless after the sprint. "He angled toward the creek, but there's no way out down there. A car's got to be parked somewhere. It wasn't in my driveway."

Dave disappeared into the next room while I described what had happened. I wasn't sure he was listening, but he'd heard every word. He came back with a heavy gun in his hand—the Smith and Wesson was bigger than I expected. It was another sign of the violence that had invaded our lives.

"He could still be in the woods if he doesn't know his way around. Especially in the dark," Dave said and held up an industrial strength flashlight as menacing as the gun.

"What are you going to do?"

"Find the bastard. You stay here." Dave said over his shoulder.

"Don't—"

He was already out the door. Slush and loose gravel skidded under his boots. The noise of his feet sounded hollow in the snow. He didn't look back.

A shootout on Mountain View Road was not the solution I'd envisioned. I should have known that a guy who advertised his gun on his bumper wouldn't be content to stand still and let me hide behind him. But I couldn't tolerate not knowing what was happening and crept down the hill at a safe distance.

I kept to the shadows. The snow was ankle deep, more so in some places, and sheets of ice slid off the branches of the shrub row as I brushed past. I caught up with Dave at the bottom of his driveway. Across the road, where my house was tucked behind a pair of cedars, the evening seemed peaceful. Everything was quiet except for the blood pounding in my ears.

"This has to do with Martin," Dave said. "That's where I'm going." He stood in a bent-kneed posture, like an animal ready to pounce. Then he turned out his light, crossed the road and crouched in the underbrush alongside Martin's driveway. The night was black and Dave's khaki work pants disappeared into the duff. In spite of the dried-up scrub growth, he moved silently. I didn't hear another sound.

A moment later, I heard the shrill of tires on gravel and the crack of gunshots. One hit metal and echoed in the night. A dark-colored car peeled out of Martin's driveway and fishtailed on the slick pavement.

Dave sprinted back. "I'm getting the truck," he whispered in a voice that sounded disembodied.

"Stop it," I screamed. "This is out of control."

But Dave was already in his truck and skidded away, spraying me with a wake of dirty snow from his tires. I stared at the empty road where he had disappeared and crossed back to my house. I was halfway up the driveway when the King County Sheriff sped up with red lights flashing. He jumped out of the car with his gun drawn and pointed at me.

"Hands up!" he yelled.

My hands shot up. The sheriff was young and nervous and very serious. Before he could lower the gun, lights flashed behind him and another car skidded up. The Duvall Police had arrived.

The cruiser's headlights pinned the young crew cut sheriff in its beams. Thank god I knew Carl Ring. He leaned his meaty shoulders out of the cruiser and pulled himself up in slow motion. "I think this would be Duvall jurisdiction, not county."

"County," the younger man said in a reedy voice. "County jurisdiction starts at Mountain View."

"This is part of the murder investigation in Duvall. And you're aiming that gun of yours at the woman whose house was broken into."

Before the young sheriff could respond, Frank pulled up in his battered station wagon. He left the rear end of the car hanging out of the driveway. It was crowded with the official cars. Dave Bender followed and abandoned his car in the middle of the road.

The County Sheriff was probably twenty-six, but looked sixteen. He'd drawn a big audience with all the commotion and he still hadn't put the gun down.

Frank pushed up to him. "Jesus Christ, put that gun down. Somebody better tell me what's going on."

The sheriff's gun hand trembled a little.

Carl Ring had a son Nell's age and he responded to the young man like a father. He walked over and touched his arm. The kid lowered his weapon and holstered it. Carl turned to me. "Now, what happened, Grace?"

I told the story, the kicked-in door, the crash from Nell's cabin, the man.

Dave added the story of his chase down to Kelley Road. "But I got tied up at the community center. The goddamned drumming group was just letting out. There were fifteen people loading African drums into dark cars that looked just like the one I was following. They pulled out onto the road in front of me."

"What was the make?" Carl asked.

Dave and I looked at each other. Neither of us knew.

"License plate number?" Carl asked but didn't sound hopeful.

"Couldn't get close enough. But I think I hit it when I shot."

Carl looked like he didn't want to hear it, but somewhere, a dark sedan had the bullet hole.

We reached the back porch and inspected the damage. There were no other signs of disturbance. I couldn't have known something was wrong from the front.

Dave led the way to Nell's little house. I turned away when I saw her door kicked open. It hadn't been locked; the intruder just hadn't bothered to check. The crash had come from the sitting area where we watch TV, a reminder of the scene I'd found at Martin's. The television lay on the floor, belly up like a turtle, the glass broken in a pattern of vertical jags. The combination VCR and DVD player was still there, but our small collection of films was scattered on the floor with broken discs and ribbons of tape ripped from old plastic cassettes. I knelt to pick up a crushed tape we had made with the camcorder. NELL'S FIRST STEPS was penciled on the label.

"What if Nell had gotten home this week?" Worry disguised as anger played across Frank's face.

Now I was glad I had told Nell to stay in Mexico. "Someone broke this on purpose. I don't even think anything is missing."

The willful destruction was senseless, worse than burglary. The movies had captured the innocence of Nell's childhood. The ruin punctuated every loss of the past three days.

The four men crowded into the tiny room with gray snow puddled at their feet. I made my way to Nell's bedroom. Windows circled the walls and made the room feel a part of the woods. Glass doors opened out onto the deck at the water's edge. When the sun was shining, light shimmered on the ceiling, reflected by the pond. That sense of peace was shattered too.

The doors hung open. I flicked on the outside light and saw sliding footprints in the thin layer of snow on the deck. Scuff marks in the snow at the edge of the pond led into the woods. There was no path; the leafless branches of salmon berry and currant were snapped off and pulled away.

Carl took charge. "Frank and Dave, you know the woods. Follow tonight's trail. Look for anything he dropped and see if you can figure out how well he knew the way." Carl sighed and looked at his young colleague from the Sheriff's Department. "What's your name, son? We haven't met."

"Wayne Paiges, sir." The young guy stood up straighter and looked even younger, if that was possible. They seemed to be slipping into some kind of law enforcement hierarchy in which Carl was the kindly but tired older man.

"You go with those two and collect any evidence. Got everything you need?"

Wayne took off at a trot to collect flashlight and evidence bags from his car. I wasn't sure if Carl expected him to find something, or if he had given the kid a job to keep him busy.

Carl continued, "Grace can show me the usual path. We'll see if it's been used tonight. The snow will help. We'll all meet at Martin's and see if his house was entered."

Carl and I made our way through the woods. We retraced the path I had taken with the puppy on the morning I discovered Martin missing. The only disturbance visible tonight was the narrow, v-shaped marks of deer. The sound of snapping twigs and voices carried through the night air as Frank's group explored the human footprints.

We came out of the trees at the edge of Martin's property; Carl slowed his pace and swept the flashlight over the clearing. A trail through the snow broke out of the woods to our left. It led through Martin's rose garden and toward the driveway. Carl and I walked alongside the path, not wanting to obscure anything important with our own steps. The garden arced along a terraced stone wall where the property sloped down toward the house. This early in the year, the thorny bushes were bare, but drifts of lavender-veined crocus poked up through the snow visible in the beam of Carl's flashlight. A boot had crushed them.

The runner hadn't anticipated a drop-off at the wall. He had fallen. The flattened drift reminded me of the snow angels I'd made as a kid, spread out on my back, sweeping my arms to make wings. The steps scrambled off again and stopped at the tire tread that marred the snow where a car had been parked. There was no sign of entry at Martin's house. We followed a line of footprints beside the tire tracks that led down the driveway. He must have walked the long way to my house earlier, staying hidden in the bushes at the side of the road. I hadn't noticed the footprints in my driveway when I ran to Dave's house in the dark.

"Pretty sure this was the same person that broke into Martin's house," Carl said.

The days with unbroken tension erupted in me. "And killed him. What are you doing about this? Did you find out anything about those bones?"

Carl's expression said no. "You know I can't talk—" His preplanned denial dropped off. Then my question hit home. "What bones?"

"The ones Gwen brought in from Martin's shed." A beat later, I realized that he really didn't know.

Carl came to a full stop beside the snowy tire tracks. "There's no one brought any damn bones in," he said. "What kind of bones?"

Chapter 12

THE FROZEN TREES creaked in a gust of wind and Carl turned his collar up against the cold. I suddenly felt very tired. I had only assumed that Gwen had delivered the box.

"What kind of bones?" Carl repeated, louder.

"When we were locking up Martin's house, we found a box in the shed." I told him what had happened. "I told Gwen to give them to you. But you know how emotional Gwen was that night."

"She came in and talked to us all right. But she didn't bring a thing."

I thought about the times I'd seen Gwen since then. She'd seemed to be coping well enough when we planned the memorial. She knew from the county council meeting that grave desecration was an issue. And she still didn't take the bones to the police. I'd believed that I didn't need to worry about Gwen quite so much. I was wrong.

Carl turned off the flashlight and hung it from a loop on his belt. The snow reflected enough light for us to see the way as we walked again, side by side along the tracks. We were almost back to Martin's house. Three lights bobbed at the edge of the woods.

"I'll get those bones for you tonight," I said. "I dropped some things off at the station earlier today too. Did you get them?"

"That bag of Mallecke's things and the disc," Carl's voice got gruff. "You're as bad as Gwen. It only now occurs to you that the film he just finished might be of interest to the invest-tigation?"

I didn't answer.

"Look at your television and videos back at the cabin. It's occurred to someone else too. Who knew you had the film?"

"Anyone Martin might have told. Frank and Gwen. Lydia Taylor. She showed up at Martin's house looking for his films."

Carl shoved his hands into the pockets of his khaki uniform jacket and shook his head at my gaffe.

The lights from Frank's group swung out by the rose garden,where the runner had fallen. The cloud cover broke up and a weak moon rose over Martin's unlit house throwing indistinct shadows on the snow. Across the clearing, the flashlights paused and clustered near the garden wall. An excited "Look here!" carried through the night air.

Wayne jogged up holding a plastic bag with a torn piece of cloth inside. Carl shined his light on the contents—a scrap of dark blue fabric, maybe Gortex. Someone had ruined one of those expensive parkas they sell in REI. The material wasn't weathered like something that had hung in the underbrush for days; it was stiff and new. It didn't add much to the glimpse I had of the burglar running from the cabin. Everything had been dark.

"Good job," Carl praised Wayne in a tone I would have used on the puppy. "From the woods?"

"A rose bush got him. That sucker had big thorns." The young guy straightened his uniform and preened a little before he passed the baggie to Carl for safe keeping. He was pleased, but I doubted anyone was going to check all the hall closets in the county for ripped rain gear.

"Anything else of interest?"

"No sir," the young sheriff spoke like he was addressing a military commander. Frank and Dave exchanged an indulgent look and let the kid tell the story. "He never hit an actual trail back in the woods, but we know he found a way out."

Carl tucked the evidence in his coat pocket. "I suppose anyone could have found a way. We may as well get on back to Frank and Grace's and finish up."

The five of us filed back through the woods. There wasn't much talk, just the sounds of our footsteps as we walked. A frosting of snow clung to the cedar shakes on the weather side of the cabin. It sparkled in the moonlight and made the burglary seem unreal. The windows glowed a warm yellow and the bamboo garden hid the burglar's damage until we came up on the kicked-in door.

The phone was ringing when we got there. I ran around the huddle of men and jumped over the broken TV to pick up before it stopped. It was Nell. I didn't have any good news for her. I told her about the burglary and how we thought it might be related to the film.

"I knew I should have come home right away. What was on that disc, anyway?"

"Nothing that I could see."

"Did you look at the cuts?"

When I didn't answer right away, she said, "Mo-om," with the two-toned inflection kids use when their parents are being backward. "The parts he cut out when he edited the film. They're around somewhere. Did you check the computer?"

"No."

"Listen, I'm catching the next flight home. Something bad is happening." Her voice took on the stubborn quality she got when she was determined.

She was right, something very bad was happening. That was why she shouldn't come home. I wanted her in a safe place. Nell's cabin had been invaded, first by the burglar, and now by the large men examining it. Her girlish treasures—the beaded necklaces she made and draped from hooks on the shelves, the bright bottles of polish she used to paint her toenails while she bent over each foot with the concentration of a fine artist—these were sullied when Carl and the sheriff pressed shoulder to shoulder to collect fingerprints. The men filled the tiny square of floor between the couch and the TV table. Carl's broad back took up even more room in the bulky police-issue jacket. Wayne Paiges squatted to check the pile of books and tapes on the floor. I flipped the phone cord out of the way and backed into the bedroom doorway.

I held the phone away from my ear and stared at it as Nell argued, once again, that she should come home. Since the break-in, I'd felt a little bit psychic in my insistence that she stay away. I didn't want to imagine what might have happened if Nell had been here, maybe napping when the glass shattered and wood splintered. "You stay for the rest of the week. I don't want you involved in this."

"No way," was what Nell said to my directive. "I can't believe you. Like I could concentrate on exams when I'm worrying the whole time. You can't shelter me, Mom. Martin is dead and you're on somebody's list too. How about protecting me from the next phone call—the one that tells me you and Dad have been killed."

I hadn't been that afraid while the burglary was happening. Now, my stomach tightened. I didn't think I was wrong to want to protect her.

"Let me talk to her, Grace." Frank reached for the phone and shook his head in an emphatic no while he listened. He heard the same argument and finally said, "I don't want you staying in your cabin, though."

I could tell she didn't argue with that. I looked around the cabin where Carl and baby-faced Wayne Paiges hadn't found much in the way of evidence. Dave Bender came back from a trip to his house with a roll of heavy plastic sheeting to make a temporary cover for the broken windows. I let them all take over and sank down on the lumpy couch to watch them patch up the shattered window. Then I called Gwen and told her I wanted to see her.

~

The men in their big law enforcement coats had finally gone. I made a pile of the scattered books and tapes and shoved them under the table to sort later. I pulled the broken door shut to hide the mess and started up to the main house to join Frank.

A car door slammed in the clearing and Gwen rushed down the slippery path toward me. "Damn it, Grace. You could have been killed. Did you think of that?"

Gwen's coat was thrown over her shoulders as if she hadn't even taken time to put her arms in, and her hair stuck out in a wilder version of the usual waves. She wore a bright pair of mules on her feet. With snow lapping at her pedicured toes, the inadequacy of her shoes broke my heart. She grabbed my arm to lecture me about my imminent death and the coat slid off onto the snowy path, revealing her silky pajamas. I picked it up and guided her back to the house.

On the porch, Frank bent forward with a fan of nails in his mouth and tapped a one by four into the ruined doorjamb. He swung the door wide to let us pass.

I settled Gwen in the kitchen and brought warmer clothes. The wool socks I lent her were a rough contrast to her feminine night clothes. I dug three brandy snifters out of the cupboard and dusted them off on my shirt. I set the brandy on the table in front of Gwen before I started my lecture.

"Carl Ring was here after the break-in. He told me—"

"Why can't he stop what's happening?"

"He doesn't have all the information. You never took that box of bones in."

Gwen examined the hem of her sleeve and rolled it between her fingers. "Oh Grace, I just don't know what to do."

Today her helplessness made me angry.

"Why didn't you take the box with the bones in, Gwen?"

"I didn't want Martin to get in trouble."

"He can't get in trouble. He's dead." My tone was irritable. "You're blocking the investigation. You're the one who will get in trouble." I waved at my broken door. "And me."

Gwen gulped at the brandy and the tears started again. "I don't want his memory tarnished. The memorial is tomorrow. I'll take the box in after that. I want everyone to think the best of Martin."

The fire snapped in the wood cook stove my grandmother used before the electric lines ran to the house. I rarely lit the relic, but Frank had fired it up to fight off the extra drafts and fed it with scraps of wood from the repairs. Gwen blew her nose on a used-up tissue. She pulled open the chrome door to the firebox and tossed it in. Black mascara smeared in half moons under her eyes.

"No more waiting," I told her. "When you leave, I'm following you home. I'll take the bones to the police station myself. Tonight."

"Don't worry, Gwen," Frank soothed her from the doorway where he tapped at the doorframe with the hammer. "Martin's memory isn't that fragile. People loved him."

I wished I had as much patience. My grandmother's old kitchen was the place I'd felt most secure as a child and I extended the cocoon of safety to my family. Now our refuge was vulnerable. Sometimes I really believed that I could make everything all right again. When I was a kid, that's what I had to do with my mom. Small problems incapacitated her. I fixed them. It left me feeling too invincible.

Gwen and I left shortly afterward. I followed her old Volvo over snowy roads and collected the box. We hugged and, once again, I was struck by how fragile she seemed. Then I delivered the bones to Carl at the police station where he was still digging through a backlog of work.

When I finally got home, Frank had just finished the repairs and I was starving. I found the flashlight and stopped at the chicken house to collect the eggs I'd been too negligent to pick up in the past few days. Another omelet for dinner.

The girls were queued up on their perch, asleep with their backs to the door. The daylight stayed longer now and the chickens were laying again after a winter hiatus. The rooster was at the end of the lineup and faced the opposite way, maybe to keep watch. He rearranged his feet on the perch and looked on as I pulled the new eggs from the nesting box. The poor guy seemed diminished without his tail, a Samson without his hair. I figured that was what hubris got him.

Chapter 13

THE DAY OF MARTIN'S MEMORIAL, a pale sun came out and icicles dripped from the roofline, but I sensed another front moving in.

Frank ironed his third shirt of the afternoon. The previous two were tossed on the bed, rejected as not quite right for the occasion.

"How's this one?" he asked. The cream colored shirt he held up for my inspection was almost identical to the two he had abandoned.

"Very nice."

Frank wasn't used to wearing anything more formal than blue jeans, and he was under extra pressure today. Watching him pick a tie would be painful.

"I was crazy to let Gwen talk me into giving the eulogy." He turned the iron off. "Let me practice on you one more time."

I knew his talk by heart but listened while I got ready. Dressing was easier for me. I had one outfit appropriate for a funeral, a dark blue dress, knit like a sweater. It clung a little, but not too much. My biggest decision was whether to add a necklace or a scarf.

A part of me still felt prickly about our argument over Nell's coming home. She would be on her way home soon, but too late for her to go to the memorial. I was supposed to know about people's need to grieve—and I had denied Nell the chance. I sighed and chose a necklace with twisted strands of amber. Frank came over to fasten the clasp while I held up my hair.

I put on lipstick and pinned my hair into a French twist like the one my mother used to wear. There had been a time when I wanted to be as unlike my mother as possible. But my dress-up ideal had come from a nine-by-twelve photograph of her during the forties. She'd never looked better, with soft brown hair and Katharine Hepburn eyes.

Frank started over on his speech. I went downstairs and leaned my forehead against the cool glass in the front door. The panes wobbled in the rickety squares, but the cold air that seeped through the glass revived me. In spite of all the ironing, Frank and I were only ten minutes behind schedule when we started out the door. I balanced a bowl of salad, two bottles of wine, and Martin's DVD. But the phone rang before we got the door closed. I went back in, hoping it was Nell with a flight schedule. But it was Jo Price, a friend from Harborview. I unloaded the food and bottles on the desk.

"Sorry to bother you at home," she said. I could hear other phone lines ringing in the background. "But I wanted to ask you a question."

I held a finger up for Frank to wait and sat down in the squeaky chair by the desk. "Sure, but I only have a minute, I'm on my way to a funeral."

"Oh, I am sorry. I'll be quick. It's about the woman you sent in Thursday night."

"Liz Larkin?" I said. "Is she okay?"

"There's something funny about her."

I trusted Jo's instincts. She'd worked in psych for twenty years and had a sixth sense about what was going on with people.

"When Liz came in, she was psychotic. But this morning, she really freaked out—in a different way. She got agitated, saying someone is going to kill her because of what she knows. We hear that kind of paranoia all the time. But it sounded so specific, I wondered if she was really in trouble."

"Like what?" I said.

"Well, all this started right after she got a phone call. I thought she'd been threatened."

"Do you know who the call was from?"

"It was a man, that's all I know. She'd been doing better. Then she started talking about the gas man and explosions again. But worse."

"What exactly did Liz say that worried you?"

"She said, 'the gas man will kill me if I tell. He said he would.' Then she said, 'I can't find Alfred. What happened to Alfred?'"

My stomach dropped. "Alfred Mallecke."

"She didn't say a last name."

"A homeless man named Alfred Mallecke was murdered a couple days ago. I heard he had been helping a woman. We should take Liz seriously."

~

I wanted to talk to Liz right away but turned my focus to the memorial. Each crisis would have to get its individual compartment and wait its turn. Liz was okay. The fifth floor of Harborview housed the locked units. I couldn't count the number of times I'd told people with paranoia how safe it was there, the implication being that whoever was after them couldn't get to them. But in a sense, it was true. Every visitor was screened before they came through the heavy locked doors. Now was the time to focus on saying good-bye to Martin.

Gwen's house on Stella Street was part of the original grid platted behind town and would have fit into the film of local history. She lived in an old white church that she had converted to a home, steeple intact. Newcomers to town often came to the door to inquire about the hours of services. Today it was real. The service was at six o'clock.

Gwen looked electric. Nervous energy spiked her movements and her color was high. She took our food offerings at the door. Inside, the space had been left open, divided only by the groupings of furniture and Oriental carpets. Wavy-glassed windows let in what was left of the muted Northwest light. Weak rays angled across the former sanctuary.

Gwen and I set out the food and put finishing touches on the table with two big pitchers of the first flowering cherries from the valley. The puppy was already in trouble. Caesar put his nose to the edge of the table to sniff the delectable treats, but couldn't stop there—a paw followed.

"I can't take another day with this dog," Gwen said and pushed him away. "My cats have gone into hiding. Please Grace, take him for a while."

Frank and I did have space for Caesar to run, as long as we kept the chickens cooped up. I didn't feel up to a puppy either, especially a chicken-eating husky, but I could tell that Gwen was at the end of her rope. I agreed to take him for a week.

I enticed Caesar out to the back porch with a corner of bread and made him a nest where he looked right at home. With his thick, downy fur, this puppy was more adapted to the temperature outside than in. It was snowing even in the valley now, but the porch was dry. Caesar lay down, put his head between his paws and looked up at me with pleading eyes.

"Don't be so cute," I told him and wondered how long my week of dog-sitting would really turn out to be.

Inside, guests began to arrive. Gwen had asked everyone to bring a candle to light, but a lot of people couldn't stop at one. There were tables of pillars, counters of tapers and nooks of votives, numbering more than a hundred. With hushed voices, everyone helped light them. We struck match after match. Trails of smoke filled the room and the smell of sulfur stung in my nostrils. In the soft, flickering light, Frank swallowed hard and began the eulogy with a quote from Ezra Pound.

"What thou lovest well remains, the rest is dross.
What thou lov'st well shall not be reft from thee . . . "

I was proud of him. No one would ever believe how nervous he had been. He looked a little awkward in his suit and the cream colored shirt, but most of the other men there did too.

Frank wrapped up the speech and turned the floor over for friends and family to tell favorite memories. Bittersweet tears pushed at my eyes as I listened, but I still didn't cry.

After a prayer, people drifted into groups around photo albums laid out on a table, a screen in the corner where Martin's film played, and tables crowded with food. Friends had baked their concern into cakes and pies. Gwen stood at the food table surrounded by pots of soup and loaves of bread and platters with colorful mounds of fruits and vegetables. She layered slices of cantaloupe around the edge of a plate where they circled like toothless smiles.

A couple of neighbor guys tuned guitars to add music to the mix. No matter how Martin had died, he would want a wake in the Irish style. Lively and drunken. Under a leaded glass window, a narrow table was packed with icons and candles. I reached out and traced the carved edge of a frame that held a photograph of Martin at a late night bonfire. In the picture, flames threw shadows on his face and made his expression look wicked.

A man's voice came from over my shoulder. "The local history piece was interesting, but I wanted more. An hour on the tribe alone would have whetted my appetite. But then, I'm a history aficionado. Martin and I had something in common there."

I realized he was talking to me and turned around. It was Will Taylor, Lydia's husband. In the candlelight, he looked as handsome as he had at the community center, with a startling combination of curly dark hair, gray-green eyes and skin so fair that on a woman it would be described as porcelain. His suit jacket hung casually open. In comparison, the knit dress I had been so satisfied with before I left my house seemed to fit like a sack. I always felt dowdy around men like him, but I tried to salvage some of my social skills and struck up a conversation.

"Did you know Martin well?" I asked.

For a minute, Will looked as if I'd asked him for a ticket to the memorial and he didn't have one. Then he smiled, "Unfortunately, I only met him once, at a fundraiser for the Eastside

Theater Workshop. But I can tell he touched a lot of people. Lydia was working with him on that proposal for the theater."

He nodded to where Lydia stood with a cluster of people near the single step that led up to the kitchen. It had been the altar originally. Gwen had worked some of the altar furnishings into a half wall that marked a separation between the rooms. Lydia was leaning on a lectern and picking at a plate of food. "I feel out of place," he went on. "I don't know anyone here."

I played assistant hostess and tried to make him comfortable. "I was going for a glass of wine. Want anything?" I waved him toward the table where drinks were set up. "Do you live in the area?"

"Woodinville since 1989," he said and poured us both a drink. His was seltzer.

Woodinville was the next town east, ten miles down a road that had been lined with Douglas fir in '82. It had since won some tongue-in-cheek awards for uncontrolled growth and outrageous traffic—a good example of what happened when you didn't have zoning laws. Lydia and Will probably took it as a model for the rest of the county, but this wasn't the time to get into a discussion of our relative philosophies on growth.

We drifted back to the same spot in front of the shrine Gwen had made for Martin. Someone opened the front door to cool the room and the flames from a hundred candles jumped in the draft and made the shadows of the statuary dance on the wall. The Virgin Mary and Buddha mingled with photographs of Martin on a table lit by the yellow glow.

Will Taylor studied the shrine. "Eclectic religious ideas, eh?"

"About what you'd expect from a woman who lives in a church. Some people think it's sacrilegious, but for her, I guess it's pantheism."

"These days you have to cover all your bases," he said. He pointed to Martin's picture on the table in front of us. "Were you a close friend?"

"Next door neighbor for ten years." That quickly, the tears I had been keeping at bay almost flooded. I didn't want to cry in front of a stranger and let out a deliberate breath to regain my composure but not before he saw the wave of emotion.

"I'm sorry. An unexpected death is a shock; Lydia is devastated." His voice was thoughtful. "I lost a friend last year and still find myself coming up with things I want to say next time I see him."

I told him about my grandmother's death, how my mother and I took turns sitting with her in the final days. "Some deaths are the natural conclusion of a long life," I said. "They make sense. Martin's death didn't."

He let his graceful posture down a bit. "Not all family deaths are so intimate. My father died last year. I didn't even go to the funeral."

"I'm sorry."

"All the time I was growing up, I never knew what to expect, expensive presents or verbal abuse. He bought me a bike once and then pawned it the next week when he blew all his money. I hate to admit it, but I was relieved when he died."

"Alcoholic?" I asked.

He nodded and held up the glass of seltzer in his hand. "I haven't had more than three drinks in my life. You wouldn't believe what a challenge that was when I was in college, but I couldn't take a chance on turning out like him. When I die, I want to look back and know I led the good life."

"Not *a* good life?" I asked, emphasizing the *a*. "You mean materially or morally?"

"My father missed out on both counts." Will swirled the ice in his drink, then looked at me straight on. "So if you died tomorrow, would you be able to say you led a good life?" He leaned forward and looked into my eyes with an intensity that seemed a little too intimate.

"I think so. I've never been too idealistic about changing the world, but I've probably helped some. My family is more what I'd measure by. Great husband, great daughter. I did okay there." Assuming I smoothed things out with Nell first, but that was none of his business. "That's more important to me than material things."

"Of course it is, but that doesn't mean you can't like nice things too." Will said and stepped closer.

We were doing the dance of two people with different needs for personal space and I was about ready to find someone else to entertain Lydia's husband. I saw Dorothy Miller, who stood a little out of the way of mingled groups of people, and waved her over. A whiff of powder and lavender came with her.

"This is Will Taylor, Lydia's husband. He's a history buff." I introduced him and turned in her direction. "Dorothy Miller, president of the historical society."

Dorothy gave me a look with hooded eyes and didn't pick up the history thread. "Gwen told me that your house was broken into. I know this has something to do with what happened to Martin."

The anxiety I'd kept at bay slid back. "It was like the burglary at Martin's. Our movies were ripped apart. But let's not talk about that now."

"Are there many burglaries out here?" Will asked.

Dorothy waved her hand at him the way she would admonish a child. "Of course not. And Grace is right. This is a time to remember Martin's life, not whatever it is that's going on out there."

"Speaking of films, though," I said to Will. "Lydia was interested in that historical society piece. I made a copy for her. I wish I'd thought to bring it today. But I could drop it by your house tomorrow on my way to work."

Will glanced at his wife across the room. He started to respond, but stopped himself and pulled out a business card. "We'll be home tomorrow. Here's the address."

I took the card. "If you'll excuse me now, I want to see how Gwen is doing."

I found Gwen sitting near the now picked over plates of food and collapsed next to her. She smiled and put her arm around me. "You look like you could use some comfort," she said.

"I prefer to be the one doing the comforting. I'm not very good at all this."

"Ms. Mental Health. Can't take your own medicine can you?"

"You don't know the half of it." I told her my guilty feelings about Nell. "Let's go find someone who looks worse off than I do."

"Better yet," she said, "let's eat."

We filled our plates with fruits and cheeses but I wasn't hungry. I rearranged the food on my plate, and then I went out the back door to check on the puppy. Caesar looked warm in his heavy coat. He turned circles in his excitement to see me. I fed him all the food I hadn't touched. He spat out the kiwi slices but enjoyed the drumstick. I pulled off hunks of meat and let him lick my fingers. Caesar hadn't lost his taste for chicken.

I gave the dog a pat and went back to look for Frank. But the mood of the memorial had changed. Angry voices came from the corner of the room where Martin's DVD ran for the third time that evening. Gwen was there, hands on hips. She had targeted Bob Swan. The film was near the end, the scene at Cathedral Falls. Bob already looked uncomfortable in a too tight collar and tie. Now he leaned away from Gwen's tirade until he almost tipped over backwards. Small groups of funeral goers saw the clash but turned away, politely trying not to notice. But I could hear every word, even from across the room.

Chapter 14

"MARTIN CARED MORE ABOUT THIS TOWN than you ever will. He opposed your quarry." Gwen shouted. "Right before he died, he was looking for you, asking all over town. I think he was organizing the plan to block your destruction of the falls." She lowered her voice to a whisper that everyone heard. "But he was killed first."

An icy breeze whipped through the front door, which had been left open just a crack. The candle flames leapt again and made a silhouette of Gwen's movements on the wall. She pointed the remote control like a gun and paused the film at the same spot Frank had two nights earlier—Felix George backed by Cathedral Falls.

Bob wiped away the spray of saliva Gwen spat with her words. Small groups buzzed with questions. No one missed the implication that Martin's opposition to the quarry happened at the same time as his death.

"Look. That's what you want to destroy. You have gall to show up here." Gwen talked fast. Bob didn't even try to get a word in.

I couldn't listen anymore. I let myself out the front to get away from the scene and left the door ajar behind me. Huge wet flakes of snow blew in under the porch light but melted as soon as they hit the ground. I took a gulp of cold air and the door clicked shut behind me. I turned around, expecting to see that Frank had followed. All I wanted now was to lean my head into his shoulder, but it was Bob Swan instead. He shivered and ran a finger between the too tight collar and his neck. He probably needed to get some air too.

I felt sorry for him. "Gwen was pretty rough on you in there."

Bob slumped and stared at his shoes. He wore a tan suit that looked borrowed. "I had Gwen as a teacher in high school. What you saw inside pretty much tells you how I got along with her. I got D's in French class."

"Don't take it too personally. Gwen's intense under any circumstances—with Martin's death she'll be over the top for a while." I tried to lighten the mood and joked a little. "What did you get in your other classes?"

"Only C's," he laughed, "but I got along better with my other teachers."

I smiled. I didn't think he was dumb; something else was behind his less than stellar school performance. He'd probably been smoking dope every day since he was sixteen.

Bob was about my age but always seemed to be a case of arrested development. He didn't look much different than he had when I first met him twenty years ago, just a few extra wrinkles. His blond hair hid the gray that edged in. There were a lot of underachievers spread around the foothills, counter culture dropouts who were smart enough to be doctors or lawyers, but opted for an easier life. In our way, Frank and I fit that picture too. With a little more ambition, we'd have been the doctor and the lawyer. That's where we were headed when we met in college. But Bob had reached a level of underachievement that Frank and I never dreamed of. We were responsible citizens; he hustled odd jobs or showed up at the food bank when he ran out of money. His dad was well off but apparently didn't share. It looked like Bob would have to wait for the inheritance.

"How did you come up with the idea of a quarry at the falls?" I asked.

"The property has been in the family for years. It came from my mother's side." His eyes lit up at the mention of his project. "I used to spend hours tromping through there as a kid, up and down the trail to Cathedral Falls with my dog. It's not buildable though. The bottomlands are too wet. They flood in spring and fall. The top is too steep."

He didn't seem like the type who could only see the development potential in an untouched space, but there were plenty of those guys around. I wondered why he couldn't just leave it alone.

"But, really," he answered my mental question, "I'm getting older. I never wanted to be like my dad, playing by the rules, collecting the right house and the stuff that goes with it. But here I am, fifty years old. I just got that form from Social Security that estimates my payment when I'm sixty-five. Know what I'll get? Three hundred dollars."

The snow came down harder. He looked out at it as if he could see the elderly Bob popping open a can of cat food for dinner. I knew how he felt. A few years ago, I had been happy to get the bills paid and have enough left over for Nell's orthodontist. Now I was counting up the little pension I'd get from the county and squirreling away extra dollars in a mutual fund.

"So you and your dad decided on the quarry."

"That property is my birthright." His tone turned bitter. "And I still had to do a lot of convincing. My father never approved of my way of life. He wouldn't think of helping me out. But that was her land, not his. Mom died a couple of years ago and I pressured him to let me develop it. I was surprised, but he got into it. The quarry has been a good thing for us. I don't think we've agreed on anything since 1972."

Bob seemed to have forgotten the scene with Gwen inside. The quarry was his life. The project was supposed to repair his relationship with his father and ease Bob into the adulthood he had postponed for so long. I wished it didn't have to be so bad for everybody else.

"Did you ever talk to Martin about the gravel pit?" I asked.

Bob had hung a lot of hopes on Cathedral Falls and I couldn't help but wonder if Martin's death did have anything to do with the quarry. The hope in Bob's voice was tinged with entitlement.

"Yeah," he said. "Martin and I talked about the quarry. He didn't agree, but he could see more than one point of view. Logging and farming are played out. The only work in the woods these days is clearing the next five-acre home site for some rich suburbanite who wants a bigger house than he can afford in Bellevue. Gwen talks about traffic. They're the ones clogging the bridges, not gravel trucks."

He looked more fervent than he had the night of the quarry meeting. "You people think development's not going to come. But if it's not this, it'll be something else. And you won't like that any better."

Bob pulled back. "A lot of guys would be glad to have the work, that's all."

I wondered about what Gwen had said inside. I kept my tone conversational and asked in my most casual voice, "So did Martin ever find you? What was that all about?"

Bob's face colored up fast. "You're worse than Gwen." He said it with as much anger as she had used inside.

I backpedaled. "Sorry, I—"

The muscles in his jaw tightened. "I saw him Monday night. Big deal."

Bob hadn't answered my question, but Monday could have been the day Martin died. "I didn't mean to put you on the defensive. But why was he looking for you?"

"I don't owe you any fucking answers." Bob spun on his heel and took the steps off the porch two at a time. He strode down the icy hill with sliding footsteps and his hands jammed in his pockets. When he passed under the streetlight, heavy, white flakes spun around him like the snow in a Christmas paperweight.

~

After Gwen's outburst, people didn't linger at the memorial. The poignant spell cast by candles and memories had been broken. A distance grew between us all, and Gwen was subdued as she bade guests good-bye at the door. By 7:30, only close friends remained. Frank gave me a kiss and his car keys and left with our neighbor, Steve Warshall, to practice his different kind of coping, which would probably involve bourbon. They took Caesar along—the puppy was our worry now. Then, sex-role stereotypes intact, the women stayed and washed the dishes. We didn't talk much during the clean-up. I was on my way home by nine o'clock.

I climbed into Frank's aging Chevy, a station wagon we'd nicknamed Spotty. Haphazard splotches of primer and rust inspired the name. I usually regarded the car with humor—it was like a Jackson Pollock painting. Tonight, it was just another symbol of decay. A Pepsi can rolled under the brake pedal when I started the car. I pulled it out with my toe and tossed it into the back seat. The gas gauge read empty.

At the Texaco, I pumped thirty dollars of high test and still hadn't filled the tank. A pickup truck as battered as Spotty pulled into the next bay. The door creaked open and out climbed Richard Black. Comb marks still showed in his wet hair, slicked back into a tail, like he'd just gotten out of the shower.

The pipeline explosion in Olympia was still in the news every day. He gave me an update on his mother's progress.

"Did your brother turn up?" I asked.

"Yeah, Leonard got to the hospital before I did. After some of the stunts I've seen him pull in the past though, I wasn't too sure." Richard signaled me to wait while he took off his gas cap and put it in the bed of his truck before he filled the tank.

He continued, "He was okay about Liz's commitment too."

"Can you think of anyone who might have threatened Liz? Did she ever mention a man named Alfred Mallecke?"

"No, she's put herself in plenty of situations where she could get threatened though. That's why I hope she gets held for another fourteen days. She's still crazy as a bedbug. You probably heard this, but Liz is actually eight months pregnant. She looked so small because she wasn't eating."

"I'm not surprised."

"The social worker wants to keep her until the baby comes, to make sure she has prenatal care. Child Protective Services will probably take the baby anyway unless my brother proves that he can provide a stable home." Richard's solemn expression seemed habitual. He had plenty of reasons for concern at the moment, but I imagined his face had settled into its serious line about the time he was learning to walk. He was the kind of person I wanted to make laugh.

"Is he up to it?"

"He wants the baby. Liz wants the baby. Normally, my mom would help. But she's not well enough. Do you think they could pull it off?" Richard hung the nozzle back on the pump and replaced the gas cap.

"There are a lot of ways to be an involved parent without being the primary caretaker. Sometimes a family member takes custody, but the birth parent has an ongoing relationship."

"My brother would be a good father. He could do it as long as he stayed on the wagon. Alcoholism is nothing new in the tribe though; a lot of kids are raised by more than just the parents. Grandparents, aunts, uncles, everyone takes care of the kids. Maybe it'll work out that way."

I thought about what terrible disabilities mental illness and alcoholism are. Liz's baby faced a hard road. "Do you have kids?" I asked.

He blushed a little. "No, sometimes I think I spend too much time taking care of everybody else. You work in mental health. You'd probably call me codependent."

"I never liked that word." Then, I teased him a little, "Of course, those of us who work in mental health spend quite a lot of time taking care of other people. We get paid for it, not labeled. Maybe you could take it up as a career."

He cracked a smile. "Actually, I'm in law school. I took the quarter off to work for the tribe; the Snoqualmie are applying for federal recognition. We should hear any day that we finally won."

I had read about that in the papers but didn't really understand the issue. "What does it mean to not be recognized?"

"Recognition means treaty rights. When I was growing up, my mom had every table and chair in the house covered with reams of documents recording people's lineage, letters to senators, things like that. We had to prove we had an organized government. I used to play under the tables while Mom and Uncle Felix worked. You wouldn't believe the number of times I got swatted for knocking the papers off. Now I keep the papers and swat the nephews."

"How did you end up unrecognized?"

"Washington State history books don't explain much, do they? In 1855, the Point Elliott Treaty set up just one reservation in the Puget Sound area. That's the Tulalip Reservation in Marysville. All the tribes were supposed to move there. But they didn't all get along. Plus Marysville is fifty miles away from Seattle, so half of our people didn't go. The feds promised another reservation right here, but it never materialized."

Snow had built up in the road now. The occasional car inched its way down Main Street. Fat flakes drifted under the roof that covered the gas pumps and stuck to Richard's damp hair. He brushed them away. He seemed unaware of the cold.

"By the fifties, the federal government pulled the plug. They revoked recognition of all tribes without a reservation. Not that the feds were very good at fulfilling the terms of the treaties anyway. That's what the Boldt Decision in the seventies was about."

"That was about fishing rights, wasn't it?"

"First Judge Boldt ruled that tribes were entitled to fifty percent of the catch—that was good." Even in the glare from the gas station lights, his face shone. "But the next thing Boldt does is say that the rule only applies to the tribes that are federally recognized. We spent the next twenty-five years in the legal system to get that recognition; that represents my whole life and my family's life before me. We've been at this since the 1930s. Approval is just a few weeks away."

"Congratulations."

"It'll be back to school for me as soon as we get the news. I'll be of more use to my people when I pass the bar."

We had finished filling our tanks ten minutes earlier. I motioned Richard into the station. Maybe he was warm with the heat of youth and passion, but I was freezing. Inside, Richard fished in his wallet for enough bills to cover the gas and half a dozen day-old donuts and offered me one. I was starving. I had spent the day at Gwen's surrounded by food and hadn't eaten a thing. I must have reached too fast, because Richard laughed and insisted I take another. He followed up by prying a stack of napkins out of the chrome box on the counter and tucking them into my hand. He was pretty good at taking care of people.

"I saw the newspaper," he said. "Today was the funeral for the guy with the video camera. Were you a friend of his?"

"Yeah, I'm on my way home from there now." I brushed powdered sugar off the front of my coat, unable to find the words to express my sadness.

"I'm sorry," Richard said. "He was a nice guy. He spent a lot of time around the tribal center collecting information for his film. He filmed my uncle up at the falls."

He sounded sincere, but maybe not everyone in the tribe thought Martin was such a nice guy. He had a box of bones that probably belonged to the Snoqualmie.

"Your uncle was quite a presence at the quarry meeting the other night," I said. "Have there been problems with the burial grounds? Do bones ever go missing?"

Richard's expression turned impassive. "You mean stolen."

The lights inside the gas station glared unnaturally. A dull headache pressed behind my eyes. I wanted to tell him about the missing bones, but some caution stopped me.

"It seemed that way from what your uncle said."

"Indian bones fetch a good price on the black market. They're popular in Europe. That's why I was surprised Felix said so much about a burial site near the falls."

"It was a good point in the case against the quarry."

"That can backfire. There was a graveyard out near Redmond—this wasn't ancient, only a hundred or so years old. One day my uncle went to visit it and someone had taken a backhoe in there and dug everything up. Felix didn't tell anyone about the grave robbers for months, not my aunt, not the police. He was afraid my aunt would be too upset. And he never did tell the police."

"Didn't he want to find out who did it?"

"In spite of my going to law school, we aren't always in a hurry to involve the white legal system in our problems. Sometimes it attracts more attention and gives other people ideas."

I swallowed a dry mouthful of donut and chased it with stale coffee. If the bones in Martin's shed were from Cathedral Falls, I wondered what Felix George would have done instead of going to the white authorities.

Richard's voice brought me back from the speculation. "My Uncle Felix wants to see that film."

Chapter 15

THE NEXT MORNING, a headache hit me. Sitting up in bed brought a wave of nausea. Normally, I wouldn't leave for work until one o'clock, but I got up when Frank did. I'd promised to deliver a copy of the film to Lydia. I'd visit the tribal center too. It was all an excuse to ask about Martin. Most of all, I wanted to get to work early, so I could drop in to visit Liz. I stood up gingerly and turned my head to test the full extent of the headache. I'd try three aspirin.

I'd forgotten the puppy until I heard the click of his toenails downstairs on the kitchen floor. Caesar bounded upstairs and in an excess of enthusiasm, hopped up onto the bed where he planted his front feet on my chest. I decided training would start soon.

I went downstairs to feed and water him and took him outside to chase tennis balls before I left the house. Caesar's energy made me tired. Frank promised to stop home at noon to let him out. I was on the road by ten o'clock, figuring that a dog couldn't do that much damage to the house in two hours.

Lydia's subdivision was called The Vineyard. The development was close enough to the Ste. Michelle Winery to justify the name, but there wasn't a grapevine in sight. I cruised around the curving roads looking for Chardonnay Place. Every house looked pretty much the same.

The houses were a vintage built in the eighties. It was not a very good decade. Each had a roof-high entryway and a three-car garage. There had apparently been two choices of wood stain available to new owners: moss gray and dull green. They all seemed too big on their acre lots with limbed up fir trees. The landscaping was the sort that made me hate rhododendrons, unimaginative clumps of evergreen shrubs underlined with shredded bark. The adventuresome gardeners in the neighborhood had some daffodils coming up.

I found Lydia's house halfway down the street. A carpet cleaning truck idled in front of one of three identical garage bays. A long suction hose snaked from the truck and through the open front door. I knocked, waited and then knocked again. A high-pitched whine from the truck drowned my attempts to raise attention. Next, I stuck my head into the entryway and called louder. "Hello?"

That worked. Lydia's head appeared around what I assumed to be the kitchen door. Wet carpet with straight rows of the machine's passes extended that far, where the flooring turned to vinyl. "Come in through the mud room," she yelled back. "I'll put the garage door up."

I turned back to the driveway and the closest door started up automatically. Lydia met me and led me through the garage, neatly lined with shelves of garden tools and chemicals, into the mudroom that had probably never seen a speck of dust, much less actual mud. I thought I should wipe my feet on the throw rug at the entrance, but it was a thick weave with bright blocks of color and looked too fine to walk on. We entered an open kitchen and living area with ceilings so high that the furniture was dwarfed.

"I have to finish up here," she said and turned away to finish putting stamps on a stack of envelopes on the kitchen counter. She hadn't offered me a seat. I wouldn't have been too anxious to talk to her either, but I wanted to know about her drive to get the film.

We were saved from an awkward silence when the mud-room door opened and her husband walked in. "Hi, Lydie. I had time for lunch and thought you might be here with the carpet cleaners," he called out as he came around the corner. Will

Taylor looked surprised when he saw me. "Ah, my friend from the memorial."

Lydia smiled over her shoulder and began to fuss with a sleek German coffee maker. "Hello, dear. I was just making some coffee for Grace."

That was news to me, but I was glad if Will's intervention warmed Lydia up enough to talk. "Do you work close by?" I asked. He looked like a combination business and working man, with a shirt and tie under his bomber jacket. He carried a briefcase as well as a hard hat.

"I work all over." He raised his voice to be heard over the background noise of the carpet cleaner in the next room. "I do soils engineering, private contracting now. I rent myself out for site evaluations."

"For construction?" But I remembered the last time I heard of a soils engineer—at the quarry meeting. Bob Swan said he'd hired one to check the status of our water table.

"No, mostly I do natural resources, mining and trans-portation."

I wondered if Will knew anything about a quarry like the one planned for Cathedral Falls, but Lydia derailed the con-versation in a too-bright tone of voice. "I've been married to him for fifteen years and still don't know what engineers do." She was half-dressed for her own work in expensive-looking wool slacks and a silk blouse she hadn't tucked in yet. It hung on her tall frame. Her shoulders were pulled forward in a protective hunch under the cranberry-colored silk. "Grace brought Martin's film."

I smiled and set the disc on the counter out of Lydia's reach. I wanted to ask about Martin's death, but her husband fussed around her, insisting that he get the coffee. Their interactions suggested a confused magnetism, pulling together and pushing apart at the same time.

I turned to Will. "Do you do jobs like the quarry at Cathedral Falls?"

He glanced at Lydia and her face was unreadable. "Actually, I evaluated that site for the Swans."

"With Lydia sitting on the county council?" I asked. "Isn't that a conflict of interest?"

"I'm just a consultant. I ran some tests on soil samples and sent a report."

We both knew the results of those reports could have a big influence on the outcome. The county council would ultimately decide if the quarry was approved. I didn't want to antagonize them so early in the conversation and almost let it go, but I shook off my politeness. "I'm probably not the only person who would wonder if the Swans would pay extra for a favorable report and an in with county council."

Lydia blanched. "You can't think that Will and I would take—"

"She's right," Will said. "With you on the Council, my consulting for the Swans is a stretch of the rules."

Lydia glared at him. She probably wanted to stay the course with denial.

"We owe Grace some thanks," he said. "This job has turned out to be anything but regular. The Swans should hire a new consultant right away. I'll talk to them."

Will should have been the politician instead of Lydia. He had the skills for it. Instead of getting defensive, he turned to damage control. I was sure the new consultant would be every bit as favorable for the Swans. They wouldn't hire someone who wasn't. That was just business, not illegal.

I changed the subject and pointed to the DVD. "How are negotiations for the theater going?"

"Very well," Lydia balanced on the edge of a tall chair at the faux-granite counter. "The historical society wants their little museum but can't get the cash together. The idea is to get funding for a theater and include the museum."

"Where does that money come from?" I asked.

"King County Arts has a grant, but it's not enough. I approached several of the housing developers for help. The county council could negotiate on zoning requirements in exchange for cash contributions."

I saw where this was heading; she would trade away our open space and farmland protections. Had Martin been wheeling and dealing to get the theater he wanted? "How did you get involved in the theater project?" I asked Lydia to keep her going.

Will answered for her. "Lydia and I are both frustrated actors. That's how we met, playing bit parts in the Issaquah Theater. *Candide*, wasn't it, Sweetheart? Though these days, we are more patrons than players—"

The telephone interrupted him. Will picked up and listened, then turned his back and talked in tones too low to hear. Lydia told me that she had studied theater arts in college but watched her husband from the corner of her eye.

He put the receiver back in its cradle on the wall. His congenial expression had stiffened. "I have to be going."

"Who was it?" Lydia asked.

"One of my jobs. The company is in trouble and might pull out. I've already put in hours of work that they haven't paid for. They mentioned bankruptcy—I'm sure I wouldn't be the first on the list of their creditors to be paid."

"Are you going to be home for dinner?" Lydia murmured, barely audible even though the carpet cleaner had moved upstairs now.

"Who knows." Will's casual ease disappeared. His gait seemed awkward when he left through the mudroom.

"What next?" Lydia said. I was afraid she'd retreat to her haughty manner, but she bowed her head over her empty coffee cup. "Things haven't gone well since Will began working for himself. He spends so much time finding jobs, but he can't get them to pay. Please don't think we took a bribe from the Swans, though. It's just that he needed work."

Lydia looked up at me. She had dropped the attitude. "I haven't felt right since Martin's death. Has it affected you so much? I can hardly eat. I wake up in the middle of the night in a panic. Is that normal?"

"Martin's death wasn't normal," I said in a quiet voice. She was more likable when she let down her guard. "I've had trouble eating too. Normal grief can do that. But Martin's death was unexpected and unexplainable. Sometimes it's all I can talk about, to Gwen, to my husband."

"Right." she said. "Only I don't have anyone to talk to. Will doesn't understand, he can't, I can't . . . " Her voice trailed. She fidgeted with her cup, turning it on its side and watching a single drop of liquid run toward the lip.

I gently took it from her and poured us both half a cup. "He seemed concerned about you."

"How can he understand? He only met Martin once. To Will, Martin was just some business acquaintance of mine. He thinks I should just get over it." Lydia stood up and set her half-full cup of coffee in the sink.

"You seem to have been close to Martin."

I thought Lydia had a secret. I pictured myself talking to a client at work and held back how much I wanted to know. I remembered a counseling text that advocated leaning forward with hands on knees to show active listening. But there's no quicker way to get someone to close up. If someone has a secret, they are afraid of your response. They want to sneak it in. They hope you won't notice.

She turned away, smoothing imaginary wrinkles from her blouse. Her eyes were moist but she didn't say a word.

I visualized myself leaning back, with my hands as far from my knees as possible.

She turned toward me. The tears spilled down her face. "We were in love."

Chapter 16

LYDIA RESTED HER HANDS on the edge of the kitchen sink and didn't attempt to brush away her tears. Now that she had confessed, she was frozen. The carpet cleaner upstairs whined. The worker's steps sounded through the ceiling above our heads. I let out my breath and felt my chest sink. "You really can't talk to your husband."

Her hands wandered down to the hem of her shirt and folded it into little pleats that would never be seen when she tucked it in. "I'm a married woman. I haven't told anyone. I don't think Martin had either."

She was ready to talk. Now any old question would do. "How long had you known Martin?"

That apparently wasn't where she wanted to start. "Will and I have been married for fifteen years. People always find it hard to believe that he was my first love—at twenty-five. I was such a serious student, always good at my work, but men? I was a gawky girl and too reserved to attract much notice. That's what I loved about acting, I got to be someone else." Lydia's eyes were focused on a spot just below the ceiling, as if she were watching the movie of her youth there. "I had a few dates in college, but they were disastrous. I couldn't believe it when Will paid attention to me, then called and asked me out. We could talk for hours. He's a very intelligent man."

And very handsome too, I thought, but this wasn't the love story I wanted to hear.

She sighed and pulled her gaze down from the ceiling to where I sat. "That's not what you asked."

"That's okay." Lydia could tell it from the beginning if that was what she needed.

"We were married within a year," she said. "Our careers flourished. But everything was always about Will's vision of how life should be. This house," she motioned around the cavernous kitchen and family room. "We never had children. Will thought they would interfere. But underneath it all, I think he was afraid that he would turn out like his father. Who lost everything."

Lydia walked back to her stool at the counter. Her frustration with Will played across her face. Then she told the part of the story I had been waiting for. "I met Martin two years ago at a meeting. Maybe you were there."

I remembered a few zoning committee meetings, but no image of sparks flying between Martin and Lydia came to mind.

"Well, we always seemed to run into to each other after that. At the library, at the Safeway. We both liked to shop late at night. It seemed so innocent at first, talking over the produce." A little grin that looked almost devilish slid onto her face. "I found myself needing groceries at night more and more often."

Lydia rearranged herself on the stool to get more comfortable. She seemed softer, less controlled. "Martin brought out sides of me I hadn't expressed in so long. I even thought about taking up acting again. With Will, it has to be the board of directors or something, as far as theater is concerned. He considers it living in the real world—as if creativity isn't real. But it's not all Will's fault; a part of me wanted the power too. Not to the exclusion of everything else, though."

We sat without talking for a few minutes. Lydia brushed tears from her face then rested her hands on the counter in front of her. I reached over and covered her hand with mine. "Does Will know this?"

She shook her head. "Believe me, I'd know if he did."

The carpet cleaner finished and Lydia stood up to see him out. I thought Martin and Lydia were an unlikely couple. He had been twenty-some years older, and lived a country life compared to Lydia's suburban one. Lydia might be questioning her place in the world now, but I doubted that their relationship would have ended up as much more than a catalyst for change in a stagnant marriage. When Lydia came back, my question seemed to have stirred her concern. "Do you think he told anyone about me?"

"I don't think so. I haven't heard a peep of gossip around town."

"I suppose I'd have been forced to give Martin up someday." She paused. The softness in her face began to tighten back up. "You can see I don't want what we talked about today to become common knowledge." Now she clipped her words and her voice let me know that she was erecting the businesslike guard.

"Common knowledge meaning what?"

"You can't tell anyone that Martin and I were involved."

This was the Lydia I knew and loved. "What about the police?"

"I already talked to them."

"And omitted mountains of information. What if you know something that could lead to the killer?"

"I don't." Lydia turned her back to me and tucked in her blouse. She walked toward the mudroom door as if she expected me to follow.

I planted my feet. "Lydia, people tell their lovers things they don't tell other people. Martin had bones that looked Native American at his house. Did you know that?"

She swung around, rigid with anger, as if I had just used her confidence against her. "No."

"What did you know?"

"He told me he had gone to Cathedral Falls with Felix George to get a few more shots for his film. They didn't see anything wrong at first, but when they finished, they noticed that the undergrowth downstream had been disturbed."

"Gravesites."

"Maybe. It had all been ripped up and covered again so they could hardly tell. They were shocked, but it was late and the light was fading, so they had to hike out."

"So when Felix George talked at the community meeting, he knew someone had been digging there." I focused in on Lydia. She looked away. "You knew too."

I glanced at my watch. I had just enough time to visit the tribal center before work.

~

I backtracked from Woodinville to Fall City. Farms and wetlands rolled away from the road in emerald swaths, but the evergreens and field grasses looked limp after the cold. The snow had turned to a steady rain. The river pressed high in its banks. Fall City was a favorite fishing spot of Frank's. I hardly saw it today. Now, Lyster Oil Company wanted to locate their new pipeline here.

The tribal center was off to the right, after the business district. I passed it every day on my way to I-90. Now, I missed it three times and drove back and forth on the blacktop highway before I spotted the hand-painted sign propped by the road.

The tribal center was located in a little frame house, backed by forest, and half hidden from the road by a young laurel hedge. The way things grew here, the greenery would obscure the whole place by next year. The brown painted house, was going green with moss that the tall trees and northern exposure encouraged.

I followed a painted arrow up to a breezeway between the house and garage and knocked on the kitchen door. While I waited for an answer, I saw a group of men sitting in the dimly lit garage. Richard wasn't one of them, but Felix George rose from the circle of lawn chairs and upturned wooden boxes and came to greet me. He had one of those faces that people don't forget, with wry eyes, brush cut hair and a mole on his cheek. He carried himself well and wore the usual plaid shirt and jeans with a big copper belt buckle.

I introduced myself as a friend of Martin's and he invited me into the house. The inside had been turned into office space with long tables and mismatched file cabinets that probably came from a surplus warehouse. The tables overflowed with pamphlets and dog-eared file folders. Felix cleared a space at the end of one and then offered me a chair and a Styrofoam cup of coffee.

I handed him the disc in return. "This is the film Martin Hanish made on local history. You're in it, of course."

"Yeah, I was in it. Not everyone realizes that the Snoqualmie have anything to do with history here in the valley." He laughed. "I'm sorry," he said more somberly. "I heard he died. He got to be a friend by the time we finished."

"This has become a sort of memorial to him," I motioned toward the DVD.

Felix shuffled the DVD back and forth in his big work-hardened hands. He was younger than I first thought. His hair had almost gone white and his weathered face betrayed a life lived hard. But up close, I thought he was in his sixties, Martin's age.

"I saw you at the quarry meeting," I said.

"Grave and artifact protection is my specialty. Richard and I know what to do. Anytime artifacts are found, we just go have a little talk about legal matters. Most people don't want the expense of a lawsuit. We've shut down some big projects."

"I hope that works with Cathedral Falls."

Felix gazed out the big front window. From this vantage point, the hedge hid all signs of the road. Rain fell in sheets. The hillside beyond took on muted tones of blue-green and gray as the clouds blew in front of the dark cedar forest. "I have mixed feelings when a grave site is found. There's a connection to my ancestors whenever I touch something we've found."

Felix opened a file drawer and pulled out a box filled with artifacts. He ran a finger over the serrated edge of a black arrowhead. The box was filled with them and others chipped from a red stone. "Go ahead, you can touch."

The red point felt smooth.

"That's jasper," he said. "I want future generations to feel the connection too. So many gravesites have been lost as the city spreads. Our ancestors and our place in the natural world are our religion. People don't understand their importance to us. That's when I start raising hell."

I wondered if he'd done that when he saw the destruction at the falls. "Martin told a friend that the two of you had gone back to Cathedral Falls for some final filming. Someone had been digging by the creek, then covered it up."

"That's true," Felix said, seeming a little wary. He hooked his thumbs into the belt loops on his jeans, his face expressionless.

"What did you see there? It might be related to Martin's death."

"It may be related to his death. It's certainly related to the tribe." He was polite, but his smile was guarded and didn't mask the anger rising in his voice. "Why would you expect me to talk to you about it?"

"You brought up the burial ground at the quarry meeting, but you left a lot out. Is that what you and Martin saw?"

"If the dig had to do with any Indian habitation there, it was illegal. It's a felony to disturb a potential archaeological site whether it's a burial ground or not."

This was from a man who never told the authorities when an entire graveyard had been dug up with a backhoe. Felix George's bearing was like a rock. Big, heavy, and unmovable. I didn't know if I should trust him or not and decided not to tell him about the bones at Martin's house. "If something Martin filmed led to his being killed, I want to know. I was his friend."

"I was his friend too, but none of this will bring him back. Thank you for the film."

"The film seems related. Someone tried to steal it."

"And all they had to do was ask for it," he said, sarcastic and a little hostile. He returned the box of arrowheads to the drawer. He gave me a smile designed to shut down any further discussion.

I didn't feel like playing this game of verbal chess. "Look, I'm afraid. Someone broke into my house."

"If you're afraid, then you should talk to the police."

The table in front of me overflowed with papers listing genealogies of tribal families and legal applications for recognition from the United States government. I wondered if there was another reason he didn't want to talk. Felix seemed to flip through attitudes and I didn't know which one to believe. I could have left it at that, but I was angry about Martin's death and about the invasion of my home. "You're right, I'll talk to the police. They'll talk to you." I turned to the door.

He let me get all the way there before he stopped me. "Is that a threat?"

I didn't answer.

"As far as I know, Martin never made it back to the falls. Neither did I. The weather's been so bad I figured no one would go until it eased up."

I waited at the thin wooden door with my hand still on the knob.

"There was no doubt in my mind that there was a burial ground. I saw the evidence. I go there every year to honor the return of spring. The winter before last was unusually wet. The bank had collapsed downstream from the falls. I found some stone tools. Downstream, there was a skull."

"What did you do?"

"I covered them back up. I left them where they were put by our grandfathers."

"Did you tell anyone?"

"No one. Until the day Martin and I found that dig. Those remnants of our past could have been found by any hiker, but no hiker would have spent the months, or year that it must have taken to excavate. This looked professional. I've seen a lot of archaeological sites. The tribe is notified about every old bone that turns up."

I didn't understand. "How?"

He made the example personal. "Say you were putting in a new septic tank for your house."

I nodded. That was a realistic scenario where I lived.

"You're watching the backhoe dig the drainage field and on the second or third cut, out tumbles what you recognize as an Indian tool, maybe a scraper blade or something larger—one lady found a carving of a human figure the size of my hand, red like that arrowhead you saw. It's your responsibility to stop digging and notify the authorities."

"What if I didn't know I was supposed to do that?"

"What would you do?"

"I'd be excited, but I don't know if I'd stop digging. Renting that backhoe for a day is expensive. Am I a felon then?"

"You'd take another scoop with that backhoe, but you'd be panning the next pile of dirt like you were looking for gold. Imagine you found more. Then you'd be really excited."

"Then I might get on the phone to find out what I had. Maybe I'd just go to the library."

"Somebody tells you the Burke Museum has experts who can identify what you have. You call them. Under no uncertain terms, they tell you to get an archaeologist to examine the site. The archaeologist gets a permit and notifies me. If it's a significant find, all work is stopped while it's surveyed. I've seen it all over the county. There was no permit for an archeological study at Cathedral Falls."

"Is everything returned to the tribe?"

"Oh no."

"I thought you said the law specified that."

"I exaggerated for effect. On federal land, that's true. On private land, if you're the property owner, you keep everything you find—except bones and funeral items. We rebury those."

"What do you think happened at Cathedral Falls?"

"The Swans must have turned up the stuff when they planned their quarry. Martin didn't think the old guy was involved. He knew Bob pretty well. Seems Bob got interested in the dig that was going on up at the Tolt River and even volunteered as a helper, an experienced helper. He'd taken archaeology classes at the UW. Spent six months working out at Ozette."

I usually thought about archaeology as something that took place in exotic places, like the pyramids or Machu Pichu, but Felix reminded me how much was going on in our own state. At Ozette, on the Pacific coast, a storm had exposed a village that was perfectly preserved by a landslide. The University worked that site for ten years. Ozette was a wilderness beach and a popular destination for hikers who wanted to get a glimpse of a dig and a quick tutorial from an interested student.

Closer to home, the Seattle Water Department found a village site when they started to build a new treatment plant on the Tolt River, just a few miles from Duvall. That was postponed for a year while that dig went on. Bob had been both places.

"If Bob studied archaeology, he knows the laws. He also knows that he could keep the artifacts anyway."

"Except for the remains of our ancestors," Felix reminded me. "Either Bob fancied himself as Indiana Jones or he was worried about a big delay in starting his quarry."

"Or both. What was he thinking?"

"Are you kidding? He almost got away with it. The underbrush grows so fast we wouldn't have seen a thing if we'd waited another month to go there."

"So what did you do?"

"I planned to have a talk with Bob as soon as we got back into town that evening. But he wasn't home. Then Martin insisted that he talk to him first. I wouldn't have gone along with it, but I had to spend the next day filing legal papers for our case with the feds." He waved his hand over the cluttered table.

The topic felt edgy. I didn't know how long Martin had the bones in his shed. Or if Felix George knew about them. "I heard he was looking for Bob. Did he find him?" I asked.

"Don't know," he said. "I can't ask Martin now."

"Did you talk to Bob?"

He held his hands out, empty. "Nope. Not yet."

Chapter 17

IF MY TALK WITH FELIX GEORGE didn't make me late for work, seeing Liz Larkin on the psychiatric unit would. Harborview's grand art deco facade was diminished by grimy windows and cigarette butts crushed into the sidewalk. Wind whipped the smell of salt water and creosote in from Puget Sound. I took the steps to the fifth floor, a small concession to health after the soggy sandwich I bought for lunch. Cracks from a recent earthquake riddled the walls in the stairwell. A chunk of plaster fell off with an eruption of dust that left the hem of my pants chalky. I licked my fingers and wiped away the powder.

A phone on the wall outside the big locked door connected me with the nursing station, and I asked to be let in. The wait seemed to take forever. Someone had chosen a cool gray-blue paint for the metal door. The hospital went through phases like this. One year the administration decided the unit shouldn't look too institutional and inhumane, so they carpeted the hallway and bolted nature posters under Plexiglas to the wall.

Last year, a new safety regulation outlawed glass mirrors, so after fifteen safely-unbroken years, all the mirrors were removed from the bathrooms and replaced with the wavy metal of the highway rest stop variety. Each smaller mirror was surrounded by four crumbling holes in the wall where their larger counterparts had been attached. Apparently, no one considered the holes in the walls to be either unsafe or inhumane. They remained unfilled.

The electronic lock finally clicked and I pulled the heavy door open. A long hallway lined with identical doors—and pictures under Plexiglas—stretched ahead. Liz was just coming out of one of the patient rooms, and I was careful to pull the door behind me fully closed. Since I'd seen her last, someone had combed and cut the mats out of her hair and arranged it into as neat a style as possible, given what they had to work with. Her hair looked like Gwen's now, still pretty wild, but socially acceptable in some circles. Liz had on shoes that were old, but seemed to fit, and a pair of leggings under a man's shirt that was big enough to accommodate the high curve of her belly. Her pregnancy looked further along now that she was hydrated and had a few days of food and rest.

Liz recognized me and met me halfway down the hall. "Can I go home now?"

She did look better, but I explained that this would be decided in court today, though I knew she'd heard that a hundred times in the last seventy-two hours. My friend, Jo, a serious-looking transplant from the Midwest with a dark sense of humor, guided us to the day room and a round table in a relatively quiet corner.

"I wanted to see how you were doing," I said. "You were really having a hard time when I saw you at the Star Hotel."

Liz's mood was expansive and her voice was chirpy. Her diagnosis of schizophrenia seemed to have a touch of mania mixed in. "I'm much better now. I know I needed to be in the hospital, but I'm ready to go home now. I can stay at my boyfriend's house."

"Let's see what the court says," I told her again. People sometimes thought that if I had the authority to put them in the hospital, I could get them out too. I rested my forearms on the table, careful to avoid a sticky smear of jelly. "Liz, I wanted to ask you about something else. The nurse told me you got a phone call that seemed to scare you, yesterday. You said someone threatened you."

The room buzzed with activity, making distraction easy. A small man in layers of sweaters pushed a squeaky walker by our table. He looked at Liz and said, "You're nothing but a Fig Newton of my imagination."

Liz followed him with her eyes. "I don't want to talk about yesterday."

"Okay," I said. "But you mentioned a man named Alfred. I might know him. What's his last name?"

She twitched and started rocking back and forth in her chair. "Alfred, Malfred, pudding and pie. Kissed the girls and made them cry."

She wasn't that much better. She flipped into rhyme at a stressful question, but Malfred wasn't too far from Mallecke.

"What was his last name?" I asked again.

She didn't respond.

Her fear and her pain touched me. "He helped you, didn't he?"

Tears welled in her eyes.

"What did he look like? What did he wear?" I wanted to be sure it was Mallecke she was talking about.

Liz still sat with me at the table, but she was a million miles away. A part of me said that I shouldn't press her with more questions. She would be able to tell me later but probably not until her mental status cleared more. I asked anyway.

"He had gray hair and bushy eyebrows. A green watch cap?"

She closed her eyes and nodded.

I wanted her to say it so I'd be sure she wasn't just echoing my words, agreeing with whatever I wanted to hear. "Can you tell me his last name?" I asked as gently as I could, but Liz could probably sense that my nerves were wired.

"Mallecke, Mallecke. My friend." Her skin seemed to lose the luster she'd gained back in the hospital. "Where is he?"

I thought hard. She didn't seem to know he was dead. I knew she suspected. If I told her, what effect would it have? I pushed ahead with another question. "What makes you so worried about Alfred? I heard he was in Duvall."

"How did you know—" Liz stopped; she seemed too afraid to say more. Jo was right—this didn't seem like paranoia. But Liz's thoughts still weren't clear enough for her to say what happened. Liz had that deer in the headlights look, afraid to run, terrified to stay. I didn't want to agitate her more.

A nurse came over and whispered that it was time for court. Liz was frozen now and two staff had to help her into a wheelchair and lock the restraints around her waist and ankle so she couldn't flee while she was off the secure unit. She followed directions as slowly as she had that night at the Star Hotel.

The hospital staff wheeled her away, and I was pretty sure Liz had been at the Snoqualmie River too.

~

My supervisor was waiting for me—for our scheduled talk. In the fifteen years we had worked together, Vera March had become a friend as well as my boss. That didn't mean this would be easy.

I stuck my head in her door. "You wanted to see me?"

Vera looked up from her desk where the remains of a late lunch were spread next to a stack of open files, the same ones I'd found on my desk last week. She was the motherly type—or grandmotherly, now that she was older. Her no-frills gray hair was combed forward in a straight line of bangs.

Vera reached across the cramped room and pushed the door closed after I sat down. This was the only space in the suite with a door, but it was usually open. I felt like I'd been called into the principal's office. Vera took her management lessons from her Catholic childhood. She ruled by guilt.

"Grace, I got statistics from the prosecutor's office last week. We're in trouble here. Our office is under scrutiny because of the number of people who were released by the court. They say the MHP didn't have strong enough evidence."

At the end of a seventy-two hour hold, each patient got an official hearing complete with attorneys for the prosecution and defense, expert testimony and witnesses—just like the one Liz was in now. The grueling process required an ill person, often in restraints, to appear in court and listen to a public examination of his thoughts and behaviors for an hour or more.

The mental health professional wrote the affidavit, found witnesses and occasionally appeared in court. No hearsay was allowed. If a family member saw the person walk into traffic, the family member had to show up to testify.

Vera's cheeks pinked up. This was going to be a reprimand and she looked embarrassed for me. "I've got a list of cases . . . "

"Too many were mine," I said.

She gave a reluctant nod. "I looked through the files. Those folks needed to be hospitalized, but if the proof isn't there, we can't hold them. Your evidence was too marginal, too often. We don't get to play God. We've got to go by the letter of the law."

I got angry. "I don't play God. I always have enough evidence for commitment. The prosecutor just doesn't like to lose cases. I only need grounds for the initial detention."

"We have to work together with the attorneys if we want—"

"Want what? To avoid making waves? I don't hospitalize people without grounds. You heard about Alfred Mallecke, didn't you? I followed the letter of the law and he's dead."

"I heard, Grace. Anyone would take it hard, having someone you just evaluated die like that. And I'm sorry, but I don't think it applies here."

"The prosecutor's office isn't always right." But I felt myself deflating. The system was big and unwieldy—and my argument wasn't going to change it.

Be an adult, I told myself. Take responsibility for your part. What I really wanted to say was—it's not my fault, I didn't do it. But that's the trouble with statistics. I did do it. "Can I review the cases?" I asked.

Vera pushed aside the crumpled wrappers from her lunch and scooted the folders across the desk. "Some were grave disability cases. We know they're the hardest to get through court. But there are still too many that were flimsy."

"I'll look them over and try to be careful."

Vera had a low center of gravity, wide through the middle and hips. She settled into her chair like one of my hens on a clutch of eggs. Her voice was kind, but firm. "Go ahead and look, but we've both been here long enough to know this in our sleep. I think it's a matter of getting too close to the patients. You bend the law, Grace. You can't save them all."

I sat silently.

Vera folded her hands in her lap. "I wonder why you're getting so hooked into people. Maybe it's because of your mother."

I looked at her, a little stunned. Everybody wanted me to talk about my mother. Frank had said the same thing when we argued about Nell.

Vera saw my face and said, "You never kept it a secret that she tried to commit suicide."

I didn't respond right away and Vera didn't step in to fill the silence. We sat in the confined little office for a few long minutes.

"Just think about it," she said.

My head emptied, which always happens when someone tells me to think about something. I promised to do the introspection just as soon as my capacity for thought reappeared. Once I got started, I knew it would play on my mind for days. I said good-bye to Vera and sat down with the problematic files. I wouldn't be leaving on time today.

I was scheduled to do evaluations in the Crisis Triage Unit at Harborview that evening. The CTU was a new unit located beside the emergency room. It was designed to handle the psychiatric patients who used to clog the ER, but the ER preferred to handle physical trauma rather than the mental kind. I walked through the waiting room where an artist had placed a huge tree trunk with bare branches that seemed to go through the ceiling. Next to that was an artificial window that showed slides of dreamy vistas. The architect had designed the entire department without windows, the artist tried to make up for it.

I entered the locked door that kept the CTU patients from leaving precipitously, then entered the fish bowl office, circled with windows, where the staff keep an eye on all the rooms from the main desk. Gus Johnson was about to give me a quick report on the people waiting to be evaluated. Before he could get started, I glanced up at the grease board where the patients' names were listed.

"Oh, no. Liz Larkin?" The evidence I'd collected on her had been rock solid, but she had been released from her psychiatric hold or she wouldn't be here now.

"She'll be on your list. She was released by the court. The boyfriend is waiting with her."

"I was the one who committed her."

"Not your fault," he said as if he had already heard about the statistics. "They let her go on a technicality. The medication nurse up on the unit missed the Twenty-Four Hour Treatment Notice and gave her an injection last night. The Public Defender didn't miss that."

Someone else had slipped up. The Involuntary Treatment Act said that patients had the right to refuse medications twenty-four hours before court, so their thinking wouldn't be clouded by drugs. No matter how ill, if the attorney found an error like this, the patient could be sent home—even if home was the streets, the temperature was freezing, the shelters were full and the person was too disorganized to find a dry spot under the freeway, much less food. I remembered a case just like that. The man was found dead of hypothermia two days later. The attorney said, "That happens sometimes. I just follow the law." Of course that happens sometimes. Some of us just found people equally important as the law. I knew I shouldn't be pater-nalistic—the patients weren't children. But, the court process was polarized and oppositional in Washington State.

Gus filled me in on the patients I'd be evaluating in the next few hours, but I couldn't concentrate on his report. He was a tall man with a voice so deep and resonant it lulled me into semiconsciousness. If Gus hadn't been a confirmed atheist, he could have been a bass in the church choir. He'd been an army brat as a kid. After a childhood of rigid rules, he swore he would never again have anything to do with a controlling institution, either church or state. He couldn't quite see the irony when friends teased him that his life work turned out to be committing other people to controlling institutions.

I guess we all had our blind spots. Mine were about to be tested when I interviewed Liz. Vera was right; I had a hard time letting people go. It probably was something about my mother that hooked me, but not the suicide attempt. It was the time the gas stove blew up. I'd been thinking about it ever since the pipeline explosion.

My mother hadn't eaten in days, and I was getting by on cold cereal for breakfast, lunch, and dinner. We had Swanson's frozen dinners for times like this, but she hadn't even gotten up to heat them. I was seven at the time and thought I was old enough to do it myself.

I ran to tell her I was cooking. She was in bed, in a cornflower blue nightdress that made her look beautiful despite her debilitating mood. Her fawn-colored hair fanned out on the pillow, freed from the usual hairpins. I stared at her delicate beauty and ran back to the kitchen without saying a word. I wanted to help.

I turned the knob for the oven and tried to light a match. The paper matches bent in my hands as I squeezed them between my fingers and tried to strike one after another without success. Even in her depression, my mother must have known her daughter was playing with matches.

Gus's voice boomed and I came back to reality. "Grace, have you heard a word I've said?"

"Sorry." I struggled to pay attention. The activity in the Crisis Triage Unit overwhelmed me for a minute.

"You're doing wonders for my self-esteem," Gus said. "Here's the paperwork. Everything you need is there."

After the court dropped Liz's hold, the staff from the psych unit upstairs had been concerned. They walked her right back down to the CTU, hoping she could be detained again. My heart fluttered with nervousness, as if this would be my final exam. The gravity of Liz's release was clear. In addition to her mental illness, she had been threatened. Leaving the hospital could be dangerous. I had to make the decision.

I found her with her boyfriend in a narrow room that was just big enough to hold a gurney and two metal chairs. Liz paced back and forth in the open door.

Chapter 18

LIZ'S BOYFRIEND introduced himself as Leonard Black. He was fuller in the face than his brother, Richard. Instead of a ponytail, he wore his hair in the shaggy Duvall fashion that came from infrequent visits to the barber. I opened with some conversation about how I'd recently met his brother and uncle. Then, I asked Liz to have a seat and squatted with my back against the doorjamb so I could look her in the eye while we talked.

Thoughts about my mother tangled with questions I wanted to ask Liz about Alfred Mallecke and the Snoqualmie River. To be fair, I had to empty my mind and focus on my evaluation. I asked them what they thought would be best for her right now.

"I want to go home with Leonard. He'll keep me safe." Liz was no longer frozen with the catatonia I'd seen earlier, but she seemed very cautious.

I glanced at him and raised my eyebrows in a question.

He pushed up his shirtsleeves. "I think she needs to be in the hospital, but I'll take her home if you can't keep her."

"I'm doing better," Liz said. "If I go with Len, I can play the piano—he has one at his house. That helps me more than anything." She ran her hands back and forth in the air to demonstrate a scale. She wasn't that much better, and any gains could be fragile if she left the hospital too soon.

Leonard put his arm around her and spoke in a reassuring voice. "The piano will still be there in two weeks. I wish you'd get better first." Then to me, "Liz got a scholarship to Juilliard when she was eighteen, but the pressure was too much. That's when she got sick for the first time. It was before I knew her, but man, she can still play so it brings tears to your eyes."

"The organ was really my specialty," she said.

I thought about the times she'd been outside of Saint James Cathedral, responding to her voices, when she had the talent to be inside making music. "I bet you were a star," I told her, then slipped back into the interview. "Are you hearing voices?"

"Yes." She was honest, but guarded. Her thoughts were probably clear enough to know that if she wanted to go home, she'd better not say anything too crazy. The easiest way to do that was not to talk much at all.

"What do they say?" I asked.

Liz looked at the floor and laced her fingers protectively over her belly.

"Do you know whose voices they are?" This was like pulling teeth.

"The people underground."

"And?"

"The underground people are disturbed. The devil will pay for his sins." She stood up and looked around the tiny room for somewhere to pace. She found it in the hallway just outside the door where she took up the pointing gestures I'd seen her do that night at the Star Hotel. "Everything is connected in God's view. I've got to save the children and pray to put the people back to rest." Her voice made a crescendo, the final word almost a shout.

The CTU staff stuck their heads out of the office to see if the commotion needed their attention. I smiled and waved Liz back into the room. She was vague about what saving the children might entail. Finally, I ran through my usual questions about eating and sleeping, a couple of problems I shared with her since Martin's murder. She was taking better care of herself. She'd eaten a sandwich while we talked and recited what she needed to do for her pregnancy. She promised to take her medications. Liz was well enough to know just what to say so she wouldn't be detainable. If her voices had told her to jump from a bridge or spend a week fasting, I could have justified involuntary commitment. But even if I hadn't been called on the carpet about my flexibility with the law, I didn't have grounds to hold her.

I was still worried though, about Liz and her baby. She hadn't been discharged with medications, so I left her to wait in the little room and walked across the hall to make sure she had both pills and an appointment in her hand before she walked out the door. Leonard Black followed me to the door of the nurses' station and said he wanted to thank me for my help.

"I wish I could have done more," I said.

"I know you tried. Richard told me about you, said he respects you."

"I like him too. He's a good kid. Well, he's not a kid . . . "

"It's okay, and everybody thinks he's good. I used to resent him for being the favored son. I was the black sheep of the Black family, so to speak, always in trouble—until I got sober."

"Have you been involved with the political work for the tribe like Richard and Felix?"

"I'd say my brother and I followed Uncle Felix in different ways. Richard works with him on the recognition for the tribe. But I followed Felix into alcoholism and hot headedness."

"Felix is a hot head?"

"He was. Don't think he's always been the wise, old elder. He did a lot of prison time."

"What for?"

"What should have been assault, but turned into man-slaughter because the guy died. This was up in Alaska. They were on a fishing boat and got into an argument about fishing rights. Felix was always an activist, but he settled his scores with his fists back then." Leonard was matter of fact as he told the story, then said good-bye.

He walked down the brightly lit corridor to get Liz. Then I stepped back into the Plexiglas office and took a few minutes to look at the files Vera had given me. Activity buzzed around me as the other staff went about their work. I tuned out the hum of conversations and thumbed through old paperwork. A few cases were questionable. Some seemed perfectly valid. But I wasn't sure about my objectivity at the moment.

~

When I got home, after midnight, I found out how much havoc a puppy could wreak while left alone in the house. I had closed off the doors to the living room to prevent accidents on the Oriental rugs. What I hadn't anticipated was that he would chew the leg most of the way off the kitchen table.

My grandmother's table. The old oak had survived three generations of daughterly mischief but had never encountered a bored husky. He had not touched the rawhide bones, tennis balls and squeaky toys—the table was a bigger challenge. I'd forgotten to ask Gwen exactly what it was that had burned her out about the puppy. I suspected that it was more than her cats hiding.

Nell was arriving at the airport at seven a.m., so we had to leave the house at five-thirty to meet her. I hustled Caesar into the back of Frank's station wagon when it was time to go. There was no way I would leave that dog home alone again.

On the road, I told Frank about my talks with Lydia and Felix George. And about my patient who was connected somehow. Frank gripped the steering wheel with both hands. The car hydroplaned across a pool of water that had collected in a low spot of the highway, but he held it steady. "You'd better get down to talk to Carl Ring. The police need to know all this."

"I'll go as soon as we get Nell settled." I stared, bleary-eyed, as the gray scenery rolled by the window in a dawn smothered by heavy clouds.

Sea-Tac Airport was a forty-mile drive from Duvall. At the onramp to 405 South, we were forced to a full stop. The line of cars showed no interest in letting us merge. We finally inched our way past the sedan with the flat tire that was blocking the left lane. Traffic opened up. Rain and fans of spray from passing cars obscured the landscape. Even with the defrost on high, the dense air fogged the windshield. I rolled the window down and wiped at the glass with my scarf.

"They say it's going to rain all week," I said. "The freezing level in the mountains is up to 5,000 feet." Yesterday, the lower hills behind our house had been glazed white.

"The Skykomish and Snoqualmie Rivers both have flood warnings." Frank took a sip of coffee from the cup he kept balanced on the hump in the car's floor. The wipers slapped at the streams of rain pouring over the windshield. "Floods are worse in the fall, though. Did I ever tell you about the time Steve Warshall and I were hiking up at Marblemount?"

"Yeah," I said, but Frank wanted to tell it anyway.

"On the way in, we crossed the river on this little footbridge. It poured all night. The tent leaked. I'd never been wetter." He paused for effect, "On the way out, the footbridge was under water. We were stuck, so I tried to cross the river at flood stage."

"How old were you?"

"Nineteen. We were probably hypothermic—you can't think when you've been cold that long. So, I hung onto a sapling and waded in up to my chest. Logs from upstream came at me in the water. I didn't know which to be more afraid of, getting hit by the wood or being pulled under by the force of the river. I still have moments when I picture myself letting go of that little tree. I never would have made it."

"But you didn't let go."

"That was when Steve finally realized he had a map in his pack the whole time. I backed out. We found another bridge half a mile down."

"You guys took too many risks. If we had a kid like that, I'd worry myself to death."

We were close to the airport, passing hand-stenciled signs that advertised parking for six dollars a day. I was already planning our route home. "The Snoqualmie River didn't look that high when we went by this morning, just the usual rise. The bridge by Novelty Hill will probably be closed though."

Frank shrugged. He hadn't been stuck away from home the time both bridges closed. I'd spent two nights on a friend's couch.

But today, even with traffic and rain, we were parked with ten minutes to spare. A crowd pressed at the baggage claim to meet incoming flights. When passengers began to trickle off the escalator from the gates, Frank and I scanned the faces to find Nell. We didn't see her until she was in front of us.

"You guys didn't recognize me." She did a pirouette and seemed pleased to have fooled us. Her long hair, which had reached her waist when we saw her last, had been cut about two feet shorter.

"It's wonderful," I told her as we took turns hugging. In spite of my resistance to her coming home, I was thrilled and somehow relieved to see her.

"You look older," Frank said and held her back as if he were checking to see if that was good or not.

Nell was right. Everything about her looked different. Her long brown hair had been lightened by the sun and cut into a gamin style that emphasized her eyes and the curve of her cheekbones. Even after a long night on the plane, she looked a little brighter, as if she had refashioned herself during the time away. The three of us watched the luggage carousel and struggled with a moment of shyness after three months of being apart. The conveyor belt wound suitcases and taped cardboard cartons around in circles until we all tried to break the awkwardness at the same time. Nell made us fill her in on the details of Martin's death before she would tell us about Mexico.

When we reached the car, Nell made a fuss over the puppy in the back seat. His coat was gray tipped with black, but on his belly, the fur was soft and white. He rolled on his back when she leaned over him, giving a mistaken picture of innocence. "Are you going to keep him?" she asked.

"No."

"Maybe."

Frank and I spoke at the same time. Frank was more forgiving of ruined tables than I was. Maybe someday it would be one of those funny family legends. But that day hadn't arrived yet.

We were on the road toward home, Nell with the puppy nestled in her lap, when she broke her news. "I met a guy. It's kind of serious."

We turned to gape at her in the backseat. The car drifted into a pool of water on the highway with a loud splash. Frank went back to his driving.

"Why didn't you tell us?" I asked. "How long have you known him?"

Nell glowed with a private smile that explained more about her bright new looks than words could. "We met when I first got to Guadalajara. They matched up local students at the university with the foreign students so we could practice our Spanish. His name is Ernesto. He was my partner."

"Tell us about him," I said.

"He's so good looking, with this long hair in a ponytail and eyes that could melt you."

"Melt me?" Frank turned and kidded her, but kept the car on the road this time.

"Oh, Dad. You know what I mean. He's twenty-five. He's in medical school. I don't know what to say. You guys would like him. Here, we picked out presents for you both." She rooted around in a colorful woven bag I'd never seen before, and pulled out books and bottles of lotion that she scattered on the seat beside her, until she connected with the gifts. Her expression turned serious. "This was before Martin died and everything. It doesn't seem too appropriate now." She held up two packages wrapped in tissue and passed them over the seat to me. "This one's for you, Mom, and this is for Dad."

I opened Frank's for him.

It was a papier mâché skeleton for the Day of the Dead—a bony man who leaned over a sawhorse to cut a board. We'd admired these figurines, which used humor to recognize the dead, when we traveled in Mexico as a family. Frank set his gift on the dash in front of him. "It's perfect for me."

"He's from Colima." She meant Ernesto, not the gift. Nell had already let the death symbolism go. "Open yours, Mom. I can't believe you took me there on vacation when I was fifteen. I'd already seen his home town."

I pulled away the wrapping and remembered how a coincidence like that takes on a special meaning when you're falling in love. My present was a little skeleton mother holding the hand of her little skeleton girl.

"It's like you and me," she said, looking up through her eyelashes.

"Hmm, that mother-daughter stuff must last to the grave." I reached back and squeezed her shoulder. "Thank you, Nell."

In the valley, water already blocked the road to the smaller bridge that crossed the Snoqualmie River. Workers, heads bowed in the downpour, put out orange and white striped signs to close the road.

Nell stared out the window. "You know, Mom. For a while now, I've been thinking that Nell is too girlish a nickname. I want to be taken seriously. I've been asking people to call me my real name." She turned back to me. "Please, call me Helen."

She said it as if we'd just been introduced.

Chapter 19

NELL, OR HELEN, NAPPED by the fire in a cocoon of blankets. Across the room, Frank nodded in the rocking chair. Rain blew in syncopated taps against the window. The scene was as cozy as a Christmas card, but I couldn't relax. I'd get used to Nell's name change in time. Eventually, I supposed I'd even get used to her letting me get close one minute, just to push away. But I dreaded it. More than that, I dreaded what was taking place around us. My sense of safety had eroded. The problem with Martin's death or any unresolved tragedy was that I wanted to do something, anything, to make things better. I wanted to be active. Frank's advice to talk with Carl Ring seemed safe enough.

Caesar bounded through the living room with restless energy, so I tossed a rawhide bone into the truck and brought him along. By the time we reached town, he'd chewed the bone to a pulpy mass.

The bland brick police station sat on Main Street, also known as State Route 203. At the edge of Duvall, the speed limit was posted at thirty miles an hour, down from fifty-five on the rest of the road. In time-honored small town tradition, a patrol car often sat just inside the city limits and waited to snag the unsuspecting motorist who forgot to slow down. The arrangement filled town coffers and allowed pedestrians to cross from the bank to the library un-maimed.

I parked across from the station and cracked a window for Caesar. Already, the cab smelled like wet dog, and the windshield was steamed from his breath in the damp air. I waved good-bye to him through the nose-smeared window and waited for a break in traffic. To the west, the sky showed a crack of blue, but a dark cloud hovered over the foothills and spat piercing needles of rain. A logging truck, loaded with raw-cut timber, sped by going fifty and sent a wave of dirty water in its wake. I jumped back to avoid a soaking. The police had missed their chance with that guy. Inside the station, I took off my coat, shook the rain onto the doormat and wiped my face on my sleeve.

A receptionist with teased gray hair sat behind a Plexiglas window and observed my attempt to dry off. "Everybody who steps in that door today shakes off like a dog." She lowered her head to talk through a space in the glass.

"March should be at least a little spring-like." I greeted her back with more weather small talk and asked to see Carl Ring.

I followed her down a narrow set of stairs to a basement room partitioned into tiny office cubicles. Carl sat at his desk, hunched over a computer screen. He hunted and pecked to the end of the sentence before he looked up.

"Grace." He tugged off his reading glasses and waved me into a folding chair by the desk. "I'm afraid I don't have any news on Martin or your burglary. Wish I did."

It hadn't occurred to me to come in for an update. "I came to give you information," I said and told him about Martin's affair with Lydia and the dig at the falls. "It's a safe bet that's where the stuff in Martin's house came from."

"Really." He leaned forward to reach for a pad of paper.

Carl wasn't as interested when I told about Bob's arch-aeological experience and Felix George's suspicion that he'd been involved in the dig. Instead of notes, he drew jagged shapes on the paper. "Now, I'm afraid you're letting your feelings about the Swans get in the way of your thinking here. Martin was the guy with the bones. As far as I can tell, all Bob wants is his gravel pit. I know you're against that."

I slid forward on the metal chair and didn't bother to hide my irritation. "Sure, I'm opposed to the quarry. But I think you'd have plenty of reasons to talk to Bob. Gwen said that Martin had been looking for him. Don't you want to know why?"

Carl shaded in the sharp lines of his drawing. "I don't know about Gwen, but don't go making judgments based on what Felix George says." He said it in his best Andy Griffith voice and laid down his pencil with an air of finality.

"I'm not making judgments. I'm raising questions. You're supposed to be investigating. You're supposed to want all the information you can get. Maybe I do want an update. Did you get a fingerprint match from my house?"

"Nothing at your house but your family's prints."

I had to ask what he'd found at Martin's.

Carl lowered his voice. "Fingerprints. You know I can't tell you anything more."

~

I stumbled over the doorsill on the way out of the police station. The gray haired receptionist said, "Careful now." I wondered whose fingerprints the police had found. I wondered if being careful really helped any of us stay safe.

I slid into the truck and suffered Caesar's enthusiasm for my return. He licked my cheek and tried to crawl into my lap. I roughhoused with him for a minute and let him gnaw on my hand in that pretend way puppies do. When I got him settled down, he sat upright on the bench seat beside me. I still wanted to do something to make things better. In my mind, getting an answer to my questions about Bob Swan would help. He lived in a trailer just a few blocks down the road. Caesar could ride shotgun.

The trailer park sat on a now-valuable piece of land between the river and the defunct railroad bed that had been turned into a walking trail. This wasn't the kind of place where crumpled Budweiser cans and cigarette butts littered weedy plots with rusting house trailers. Here, every home had a well-tended patch of grass, some with trellised roses clambering over the roofs and pots of herbs by the door. The common area included the old white train depot where the historical society met on the first Monday of each month. The Swan family owned the trailer park too.

Bob lived in a perfectly preserved old singlewide. When I drove up, both his truck and a Harley were parked in front. I pulled in behind the truck, which almost matched my own Toyota. The puppy slipped out behind me and I didn't bother to put him back.

I knocked on the aluminum door. The front porch was lined with motorcycle parts organized in neat rows on the Sunday paper. The newsprint had blurred to a uniform gray in the dampness, and rain beaded up on the oily mechanisms. Caesar sniffed and came up with a black nose. The Harley must not have been running. When no one answered, I looked up the hill toward town. It was easily walking distance. My next plan was to check out restaurants. People who don't work spend a lot of time sipping coffee and chatting with everybody else not working.

The trailer next to Bob's was just a few feet away. Its door inched open, and I felt someone peering out at me. The space between door and frame widened. and a young, dark-haired woman slipped through. She had a toddler in tow and protectively held the little girl behind her. Mother and daughter both wore loose knit sweaters in neon green that could never have gone unnoticed.

I crooked a finger through Caesar's collar; he pulled toward them. The neighbor eyed me, and the dog with caution, then spoke rapidly in Spanish. I nodded, but my high school Spanish was only used on vacation and the few words I picked up weren't enough. Nell would have been a help. I heard "*ruido*" several times, which meant noise. "*Problema*? *Cuando*?" I asked, racking my brain for a useful expression. The chance that I would understand her answer was slim.

"Sí, sí," she said with an emphatic nod. She slowed way down in her speech, but I still only caught the words for "last night" and lots of pointing to Bob's trailer from what followed. She shook her head and went back into her trailer talking about the "*policia.*" I wasn't sure if they had been called or if she meant they should have been called.

I turned back to the door. Caesar leaned into my knee, his ears at alert. I decided to see if Bob's door, like so many others around town, was left unlocked when he was away.

The knob turned right away, but when I tried to push the door open, it only moved a few inches. Caesar pressed his nose into the narrow space between Bob's front door and the frame. Something blocked the way. Through the crack, I saw the spilled chest of drawers and bunched-up throw rug that blocked my progress. I braced myself to find another home ravaged like mine and Martin's had been. My heart pounded in my ears. I expected the worst. I put my shoulder into the flimsy door and shoved until the mess inside moved a few inches and I could slip through sideways.

All the lights were on. He had taken a lot of care with the space, the furniture looked handmade. But what I saw now was far worse than the mess the burglar had left at either Martin's house or mine. Cupboard doors were open, the shelves inside bare. The couch was ripped and upended. Coats from the closet covered the floor, a box of photographs dumped on top.

I called Bob's name out of caution but didn't expect an answer. Then I stepped in carefully, trying to avoid his belongings, but the puppy scrambled right through and scattered books and papers in his wake. "Caesar, no!" I said in a loud whisper, then gave up on fastidiousness and clambered over the debris behind him. I already knew this wasn't just a burglary. I recognized the smell of death.

A step led down to the bedroom. Bob was crumpled there, his head bloodied and angled to the lower level where a pool of blood had collected like a hideous clot. He must have struggled. There were stab wounds to his stomach and even his face. And blood. A lot of blood. Bob's flat blond hair was blackened with it. His baseball cap had been knocked away, but not far, like it had hung on to the end. I wanted to right it. The only time I'd seen Bob without the hat was at Martin's memorial.

The room felt hot and closed in on me. All I wanted was to lay down somewhere, maybe the seat of my truck. I steadied myself on an edge of the overturned sofa. My hand went into something sticky and when I pulled away, it was dark with blood, thick and coagulated. Caesar's attention went from Bob's fallen body to me. Dogs aren't squeamish. He licked the blood from my hand with his wet tongue. Maybe some atavistic part of his brain thought of a fresh kill. Maybe instinct led him to lick a wound. I didn't care.

I pulled at Caesar with more force than I intended and dragged him to the door, tripping on dresser drawers as I went. On the porch, I leaned into the cold metal siding of the trailer.

The door to the neighbor's trailer banged open. She ran to me, grabbed my wrist—because I held the hand that I'd dirtied with blood away from me, at an awkward angle. The neighbor pulled me off the porch. I think she sensed what had happened. I wished we could talk, but neither of us had enough language.

Inside her trailer, we moved through too-large furniture. She led me to the couch and pointed. I sank into the soft cushions. A TV droned in Spanish from the corner. "*Policia,*" she said, like before, and put the phone in my lap. I dialed 911.

Chapter 20

I WATCHED THE POLICE ARRIVE from the neighbor's porch. Dark clouds still menaced on the horizon, but the rain had let up and the sun came out in a bright glare. Carl Ring went into the trailer first and motioned to the others. I felt detached and far away, as if I were looking at TV with the sound turned down. The officers rushed in and out of Bob's mobile home with a silent sense of purpose.

Carl stepped out and left the silent officers to the evidence collection. He walked across the tiny lawn to where I waited by the two Toyotas. Caesar waited inside my truck, his head lolled out the window to watch us.

Carl patted the puppy's head without enthusiasm and didn't say a word. He looked queasy. His voice wouldn't come out until he cleared his throat a couple times. "I'm sorry you had to see that."

"I know," I stared down at the wet grass, vivid green with the first show of new growth. "I just came because I was angry after I talked to you."

Carl's color got a little better. Our earlier conversation seemed unimportant now. I didn't even care enough to say I told you so, but then I only thought Bob was worth questioning. Someone else thought he was worth killing.

"What happened?" Carl said.

There wasn't much to tell. I had been in the trailer for less than a minute. I told him about the Spanish-speaking neighbor who had seen or heard something last night. "I couldn't understand very much. She said something about the police, but I don't think she called."

Carl looked at the woman's neat trailer. Orange calendula bloomed in a painted pot. The flowers had survived the winter in the shelter of the front stoop. "A lot of times immigrants don't call. And if they don't have a green card, they're afraid to have anything to do with the police."

"I don't think she knew he was dead. She seemed wary, not totally freaked out."

Carl picked at a cuticle. His skin looked rough and I wondered what kind of work he did around his house for his hands to be so toughened.

"Listen," I went on, "you can interview her with an interpreter and tell her that you won't ask any questions about immigration papers. We do it at my job all the time. Then, she'll hopefully be more open than—" I shut up when Carl's expression turned sour. I was telling him how to do his job and he didn't like it. I didn't care; I had my own interpreter at home. Nell could translate for me as soon as she woke up. I'd practice calling her Helen.

"Sorry," I said. "You'll handle it your way."

~

The neighbor didn't come out again until Carl returned to Bob's trailer. She carried her daughter on one hip and held an arm away from her with two mugs clutched by their handles. The little girl seemed uneasy around Caesar, so they waited for me by Bob's truck. When I joined them, she pressed a hot cup of coffee into my hands. The coffee was sweet and cinnamon-scented, the most comforting taste I could imagine at the moment.

Before the police had come, I'd used simple words to tell her what I had seen. I didn't have many words left. The bright color of the woman's sweater contrasted with her dark eyes and emphasized the concerned look she gave me. Her tenderness brought a lump to my throat. I asked her what her name was. She answered "Clara," and I told her mine.

I got my purse out of the truck, showed her a picture of Nell, and had one of those moments that women from any culture can share when they communicate about their children— with or without words. In my best Spanglish, I explained that my daughter had studied in Mexico and spoke Spanish well. Clara wanted to talk. She set her cup on the roof of Bob's truck, re-arranged her hold on her squirming daughter, and jogged back to her trailer. She came back with a portable phone that she pressed into my hand so I could call Nell.

The circumstances were extraordinary enough to wake her up. My watch said two o'clock, at least she'd had a few hours of sleep. But when I punched in the number, the answering ma-chine picked up. I wouldn't tell them about Bob on the tape, but I left a rambling message in case Frank and Nell were screening calls. Still no answer. They must have gone out.

I handed the phone back.

Clara retrieved her cup from the top of the truck. The little girl sat astraddle on her mother's hip and began to chatter. She stretched out her arms and upset the balance, trying to reach some bags piled in the back of Bob's truck. Clara pulled the girl's hands back with a whisper that I understood as "Don't touch."

I looked closer. A big paper bag—like the kind people use to send away their leaves after raking in the fall—had tipped over in the bed of Bob's truck.

I pulled away the wet paper and looked inside. At first I thought it was full of dirt, mud now after the constant drizzle. I reached in and brushed away a few loose leaves, releasing the loamy smell of the forest floor. What Bob had there was a whole bag full of bones and stone artifacts.

I pulled one out and rubbed away the debris, a two-foot long club, crusted in mud. I picked at the dirt and revealed a carved face. Next I found a jawbone and recognized others as similar to the bones at Martin's house. The bag was filled with them. Rips appeared in the wet brown paper where I pulled it back, and ragged bones poked out almost with a will of their own.

Clara stepped back and crossed herself.

Chapter 21

IT LOOKED LIKE BOB had been getting ready to take this truckload of bones somewhere. Clara looked from Bob's trailer to her own trailer and held her little girl closer. She had no way of knowing they were ancient or where they came from. I thought she wanted to run, but she inclined her head toward Bob's and said "Policia," for the second time this morning.

But I didn't go for Carl right away. I borrowed the phone again. Still no answer at home. I dug through my purse until I found the little book where I had written Richard Black's phone number. I wanted to talk with someone from the tribe, and he was my first choice. I trusted Richard.

A siren wailed and an ambulance turned into the quiet trailer park. No one came out to gawk; most people were away for the day. I held the phone Clara lent me away from my ear. Richard Black came on the line but his cell phone left hiccups of blank air. I caught enough to know that he was in the Family Grocer.

"Wait and I'll meet you." Then I showed Carl the contents of the truck and left him to think about Bob's interest in archaeology. Those artifacts probably wouldn't find their way back to the tribe right away.

I pulled into the half-empty parking lot at the Family Grocer by the old coin-operated bucking bronco. I used to sit on it as a kid while I waited for my grandmother. Once in a while, a shopper would take pity and give me a quarter. When I got lucky, the ride was slow and jerky, never as much fun as I thought it would be. I got out of the truck and leaned against the horse's cold, metal hide to wait—just like when I was a kid. Its russet-colored paint was chipped now and the saddle horn was worn bare by hundreds of hopeful, childish hands.

The automatic door slid open, and Richard Black hitched up his grocery sack and came over. "I used to ride that all the time," he said, and patted the horse's forehead.

"Me too." I bypassed any more polite conversation. "I called for a reason. Bob Swan was murdered."

"God." Shock registered on Richard's face, then puzzlement. "What's happening in this town?"

"Bob's truck was full of bones and stone tools. That's why I wanted to talk to you. They must be from Cathedral Falls." I described the artifacts I'd seen at Bob's and the bones at Martin's. I told him what Felix had said about Bob after his trip to the falls.

Richard breathed out in a silent whistle.

The dark clouds that had been parked on the horizon rolled into town and dumped rain that fell straight and hard. I felt trapped on the covered walk in front of the store. "How much did Felix tell you about the burial ground there?" I asked.

"I knew he'd found stuff there last year and covered it back up." He studied the top layer of his groceries and didn't look up. "So Bob found it too. Uncle Felix didn't tell me that."

"Martin and Felix found the place where he had dug. Then Martin died. Now Bob is dead. Your uncle told me he hadn't talked to Bob since."

"Wait a minute. Do you think Felix is involved? Forget it. Revenge isn't his style." Richard thought a moment. "But he probably knows more than he's telling. I guess it's time to go ask. He's going to be up at my brother's place all day, building a smoke house. Come with me. He'll want to know what you saw at Bob's."

Richard must have seen me holding back and laughed. "You're not afraid of Felix, are you?"

"No," I lied. I didn't want to visit Felix again, partly because I wondered if the fingerprints found at Martin's house belonged to him. "My daughter just got back from Mexico and I've hardly had a chance to see her. I've got to get back home."

Richard's face settled into the serious expression he favored. "Okay, we'll call him then." He punched in his brother's phone number. From the one-sided conversation, I could tell he was talking to Liz and that she was alone in the house. Richard's speech got a little more concrete.

I heard Richard give her a thumbnail sketch of what happened and send her out to tell the men that we were on the phone. I decided that I wanted to see Liz and make sure everything was all right.

"I changed my mind. I'll go for a while."

Richard smiled at my new resolution. The rain fell in sheets, from the overhanging roof above us. "Okay. Leonard lives up at Kayak Lake. Follow me."

We ran for our trucks.

~

The drive to Kayak Lake took twenty minutes. I spent the time questioning the wisdom of going at all, but if it wasn't safe for me, it was less safe for Liz. I had taken my own truck so I could leave independently of Richard, for my own peace of mind.

I followed Richard's taillights, which were hardly visible ahead through the rain and the spray from his tires. Halfway to Monroe we turned away from the open valley and drove into the wooded hills. I followed his truck into a small clearing scooped from a wall of western hemlock on the far side of the lake. Nothing up here got much sun. The trees were tall and close. A gravel driveway dropped down to a bowl-shaped depression where the house sat with a cluster of outbuildings. The half-built shed near the trees must have been the smokehouse Felix was building, but no one was in sight. I pulled up beside Richard. If anyone was home I didn't see them, but the weather wasn't favorable for outside work.

Richard held a newspaper over his head for protection and sprinted over to my car. I cracked the window to hear him. "I wouldn't be surprised if they packed it up for the day. Meet you on the porch." He didn't wait for an answer. The newsprint curled and water spilled onto his shoulders.

The house was painted a blue that faded into the landscape. A wisp of smoke rose from the chimney. I made a break for the covered porch. Our trucks were the only two vehicles in sight.

When Richard pounded on the door, the morning at Bob's trailer flashed back. I didn't want to walk into another tragedy.

"Damn it," Richard said and pushed the door open; like all the others, it was unlocked. "I knew I shouldn't have trusted Liz to give them the message. They must have gone somewhere."

The room was cluttered but looked safe and normal, from the cups that added to a collection of discolored rings on the end tables, to the folded laundry stacked on the end of the couch, waiting to be put away. Just an empty house where a woman with mental illness didn't pass along the information that we were on our way. I knew the information must have sparked her fear.

Richard looked around the room, his eyes finally landing on a utilitarian woodstove where a bed of coals still glowed a dull red through the glass door. "Not even a note. We didn't miss them by much, though. The fire's not out." He picked up a log and fit it into the stove, then went around the room to turn on lights. "Why don't we have a cup of coffee and wait to see if they come back."

My stomach churned at the thought of coffee, but people offered it to be polite and I accepted for the same reason. With rain drumming on the metal roof and the smell of freshly ground coffee beans, a wait shouldn't have been unpleasant. I couldn't decide if I should stay or go.

"Let me try to call home again," I said, but all I got was the answering machine. I didn't know where Liz was and I had missed Nell's first day home. I left them a very detailed message about where I was and gave them the phone number here. "I'll stay for a little while."

Leonard's house reminded me of a hunting cabin, masculine and utilitarian. Richard rummaged through a bookcase. The piano Liz had mentioned was an upright with a few broken keys, not what she would have been used to at Juilliard.

I struck the notes I'd learned in my childhood piano lessons. My playing was discordant, but the piano was in tune. I wondered how Liz's music fared when her symptoms took over. The sheet music propped in the rack gave me a clue. Tiny writing was crammed between the lines and spilled onto the margins. Her themes about the dead and the people underground were familiar. I didn't know how to sort out her delusions from the real dangers. And neither did she. I thought Liz knew more than she was able to say.

"Poor Liz." Richard looked over my shoulder at the scribbling, then held out a couple books he'd pulled from the shelves. "Could you show me the sort of things you saw in Bob Swan's truck?"

He flipped through the pages and pointed out a few photographs. "Were they stone implements? People used antlers and bones for tools too, but the soil is so acid here in the Northwest that they decay in a relatively short time, archaeologically speaking."

"That would make it unusual to find human bones then," I said, wondering if making sense of the artifacts would shed light on the other questions.

"True. As a matter of fact, if you were rich, they'd put you in your canoe and suspend it in the trees to speed your spirit to the afterworld."

He passed me the books. Each one weighed about fifteen pounds. I took the load and perched on the end of the couch that was clear of laundry. I thumbed past photographs of perishable items like baskets and woven cedar hats, until I found pages with rock. Nothing was as beautiful as the carved face I had seen in the back of Bob's truck.

"So how could Bob come across all those bones?" I asked.

"Bones are unusual, not impossible. Out on the coast, you'll find bone preserved in shell midden. That's alkaline. Out toward the mountains, bone has to stay extremely dry—like in a cave— or very wet to last. My guess about Cathedral Falls is that the river changed course over time, cut away banks, keeping things wet. It's like your compost pile. You need those anaerobic bacteria for things to rot— they don't work under water."

"You know a lot about this."

"The archaeology? Yes. It's a way to connect with the past. We lost so much in the last hundred years. Families got split up. The government sent all the kids away to boarding school where they were forbidden to speak the language. Our history was passed on through stories the elders told around the fire in the winter. It was bad luck to tell stories in the summer and that's when the kids were home. So much has been lost—to alcoholism, to crime. Anyway, these old things fill in some of the blanks.

"I know a story about Cathedral Falls, though." He glanced at the window where a gust of wind sent a patter of rain against the glass like a handful of pebbles thrown to get our attention. "It's pretty much still winter. I can tell you."

I balanced on the lip of the couch near the fire and gave myself five minutes to wait. Then I would go home and keep trying to reach Liz from there. Richard was too young to be the storyteller, but I gave him my attention.

"Coyote was the Trickster, but he always helped our people. In the beginning, people in the valley were hungry and weak. The rivers and streams were full of salmon, but no one knew how to catch them. Coyote decided to make a waterfall where the fish would rise to the surface before they continued up-stream." Richard paced across the threadbare Oriental rug as he spoke.

"Coyote began his work at the first hill, but the stream was bordered by steep banks. He wasn't satisfied and left. That's where the gravel bar is today. He tried again where the river splits at the narrow island. But Coyote didn't like it there either. The rapids show where he began that work."

The sound of a car on the gravel driveway interrupted the story. Richard pulled aside a curtain and looked out.

"I'm glad we waited. They're home." He dropped the curtain and fell back into the story.

"When Coyote came to the third place, he liked it better than all the others. And there he built the waterfall. You know it as Cathedral Falls today. There the salmon leapt to the surface to climb the falls and our people learned to spear them. No one was hungry again."

"That's it," Richard said to the sound of boots on the front steps.

The door swung open and Leonard and Felix came in with lowered heads. They shook the water off their rain-flattened hair. Leonard stepped forward and grasped his brother's arm. "Have you seen her?"

Richard frowned. "What?"

Leonard dropped his wet coat to the floor where he stood. "Liz. She took Felix's van and she's gone."

Chapter 22

THE FRONT ROOM OF THE CABIN smelled of wood smoke and the wet air that came in on the men's clothing. A fire snapped in the stove. Leonard and Felix stood at the door, ready to run out again. Then everyone looked at me.

"What should we do?" Leonard directed the question to me, the expert he had met during his visit to Harborview with Liz.

Felix, like the others, watched for my response. For some reason I couldn't identify, I wondered if the fingerprints in Martin's house had been his.

"What should we do?" I repeated Leonard's question, stalling for time to think. I wanted to tell them that my work with the mentally ill didn't qualify as experience in missing persons but realized that I did know what to do. I asked them if she'd given any clue as to where she might go.

Leonard answered. "She still talked about praying for the children, but not constantly. She mentioned playing music and the cathedral. She used to spend a lot of time there. I don't know if that helps any."

"Saint James Cathedral?" I said, remembering where I'd first met Liz. It seemed as good a place as any to start a search. Felix and Leonard had already driven around the Kayak Lake area.

The Seattle Police Department wouldn't accept a missing persons report until someone had been gone for more than twenty-four hours. But I had an in with the department. For the past year, I had provided them with training on mental illness.

I learned that working with the police was a mixed bag. First, I had given a workshop to their Crisis Team—the men and women who respond to dire situations such as talking someone down who threatens to jump from a perch on a bridge or high building. Later, I developed a class that was offered to the department at large.

Most of the time, I found myself preaching to the choir. The officers who elected to learn about mental illness were the ones with the best natural skills anyway. Since the training wasn't mandatory, a percentage of the force still based their decisions on misinformation. I kept an informal tally of my progress by noting a slow decrease in the number of officers who said "He's a mental" using a deriding tone when they referred to a person with psychiatric symptoms.

The police were understandably nervous about dealing with psychotic men—a group more likely to carry weapons. Being poor and black didn't help either, but mental illness doesn't discriminate. White guys with rich families got sick too. A few months ago, I had evaluated a man from an expensive Mercer Island neighborhood, an enclave for the rich where big waterfront houses were set in a maze of curved roads that guaranteed a stranger would be lost for hours.

A concerned citizen had called when he saw his neighbor piling all his furniture in the front yard. When the police arrived, the man was muttering that someone had contaminated it with a virus. He never made a threat and didn't have a weapon. But he was a big healthy guy who looked like he worked out. The police shot him in the face with a rubber bullet. He lost an eye. I felt for the police—they thought he was dangerous and they acted accordingly. Since law enforcement officers face those decisions every day, I thought their assessments would be better if they knew more about mental illness.

Most people with mental illness don't have the money or the support system to litigate when misjudged or injured. But this guy did. He had grown up in the neighborhood and was well-loved. His father was also the head of the District Attorney's Office. The subsequent lawsuit cost the department a fortune.

My training sessions with the department began to fill up as a result of that incident.

A ninety-five pound woman like Liz didn't have as much to worry about. She might not be treated with the utmost respect, but the police probably wouldn't hurt her. I hoped I knew enough people at the department to get them searching for her right away.

I tried to organize Leonard and Felix to write up a description of what Liz had been wearing, the timing, and the specifics on the van to give to the police. Felix balked.

He paced in a narrow circle by the front door and grasped a set of car keys, Leonard's I guessed. "We don't have to get the police involved. Leonard and I can go there ourselves."

His reaction didn't reassure me. "They can check out Saint James in ten minutes," I said. "It'll take you forty-five just to get downtown."

"I won't involve the police in something I can handle myself."

"I will," I said, not letting him intimidate me. "We need to find Liz. The police can help and I intend to use them. Now, what was she wearing?"

Felix glowered. Leonard kept his eyes lowered and voice quiet in deference to the older man, but answered by pointing to the coat rack by the door. A small-sized parka still hung there. "She didn't even take her coat, Felix."

The room was quiet except for the sound of rain outside and the logs settling in the wood stove. After a long minute, Felix capitulated. He was the one who answered the questions. He needed to keep that much control. Liz had gone out in nothing but a pair of leggings and a yellow flannel shirt. The March weather felt almost balmy at fifty degrees. She'd be okay if she stayed in the van, but she'd be soaked and chilled if she was outside—and so would her unborn baby. I explained my concerns when I called in the information.

Bob and his truck full of bones seemed far away, as if they existed in a different world. Leonard couldn't stand the waiting and decided to drive to Seattle anyway. I was relieved when

Felix decided to go along. Even if Felix had been the one to threaten Liz, I hoped he wouldn't pose a danger with Leonard there. Richard would stay at the house in case Liz came back on her own.

I used the phone to call home again. Frank picked up on the third ring.

"Where were you?" The panic in my voice surprised me.

"We went over to Gwen's. Nell couldn't sleep. She's been talking about Martin's death. It's like she has to check everyone to make sure they're okay."

"I should have been there," I said.

"Gwen's coming for dinner," he told me. "You'll have plenty of time to catch up."

I expected to have the news of Bob's murder tumble out— everyone wasn't okay. But it was better told in person. I told him I'd be right home.

Richard promised to call me as soon as he had any news of Liz, but I knew I'd probably be so worried that I'd call him first. Then I climbed into my truck and wiped off the foggy windshield caused by Caesar's wet coat and breath. The puppy slid on the vinyl seat when I put the truck into gear, and he scrambled to regain his balance. I put a hand out to steady him and followed Leonard's car out of the driveway and back down the series of curves from Kayak Lake to Route 203. At the main road, he turned right to pick up the freeway in Monroe. I went left toward home.

~

A fine mist shrouded the valley in a typical Northwest gray. On a clear day I'd have a view of Dorothy Miller's Jerseys, heavy with milk, as they lumbered to the barn. To my left, I'd see Cathedral Falls. But I was isolated inside a gray cloud. I couldn't see the pullout for the waterfall until I'd passed. A forest service gate blocked access, but there was room for a couple of cars off to the side. Hikers and mountain bikes could enter on a path.

Today, the gate was blocked by a dark blue van that had parked askew. I steered onto the shoulder and threw my truck into reverse. This was the van I had just described to the East Precinct police in Seattle. The van had lots of pin striping and a FOR SALE sign in the rear passenger window.

Felix's van.

The door hung open. I ran, glad I had found Liz. But the engine was running and the van was empty.

"Liz!" I called as I peered into the van in case she was hiding.

I climbed in to see if she could be hiding in the back but saw only the unused carpentry tools that outfitted the cargo space.

I pulled up the hood on my slicker and searched the parking area. Caesar followed. The puppy leapt from puddle to puddle and shook off on me. The mist turned back to rain. Exhaust collected in the parking area; the cloud cover made a lid to contain the fumes. I went back to the van where the keys dangled uselessly. I turned it off and then slipped the keys into my pocket. I wondered how long the van had run abandoned like this. The gas tank read empty. I cursed myself for being too stubborn to own a cell phone. I wanted the others here too.

This was the *cathedral* Liz had meant. I called her name again and ran back to my truck to pick through the mess behind the seat for anything that would be of use. I planned to look for Liz. The Mountaineers Club published a list of the ten essentials every hiker should have on hand. It included matches, a knife, extra food and clothing. That was only four. I couldn't remember the rest. Stuffed back behind my seat I found a wool shirt-jacket and a plastic bag to carry it in. No matches. No knife. Yes, to half a candy bar. There was a flashlight—that was on the list. Extra water was too. The constant rain pushed the creek to flood stage; I wished for less of that. I apologized to Caesar and rushed him back into the truck. This wasn't a dog walk.

My pace was fast and I was breathing hard within minutes. The way to Cathedral Falls started on a rutted road through a wetlands. The roadbed was built up to keep it passable. On either side, acres of field grass stretched into the distance, dotted with dips and ponds. Only the seed heads showed today, with an under layer of water. The road dwindled to a footpath and turned uphill into a tangle of brush that fronted the evenly spaced fir trees. At my right, Granite Creek raced from its nexus at Cathedral Falls.

The trail followed the creek with an occasional switchback away from the water to keep the rise steady. It was dark in the woods. I had about an hour till sunset. The walk to the falls would take thirty minutes. My feet slipped backwards on the steeper grades and every level spot was a puddle. The mud sucked at my shoes and made each step an effort.

A twig snapped. I stopped. Probably a doe browsing for food. When I moved on, the sound came again, a disturbance in the underbrush.

I kept an eye on the trees to my left. My heart pounded from exertion, with a little panic mixed in. The lonely woods fired my imagination. Cougar sightings had become more common as people moved farther into the foothills, the big cats' habitat. A friend's goat had been mauled one night. Her flashlight caught the glow of two green eyes when she went out to milk. The cat sped away, leaving behind the bloody remains of its kill.

"Liz?" I called her name and lost my footing on the slick trail. Nervousness made me waste steps. I stopped to calm myself and saw slide marks in the muck ahead, Liz had been here. I found a shoe half-sunk in the mud where her foot must have pulled away. She hadn't stopped to retrieve it.

"Liz." I called again. But rain swallowed the sound as if I'd shouted into a pillow. I pulled her shoe out of the mud surprised that the little leather slip-on had made it this far. I wiped it on a pile of leaves at the side of the trail and put it in my pocket, then continued up the path at a more deliberate pace.

Only the sound of rain dripping from the trees and the splash of the creek broke the silence. To my right, white water rushed along the rocky bank and split around an island. I recognized the rapids from Richard's Coyote story and knew I had passed the gravel bar without noticing. Here, in the fall, salmon would work their way upstream to mate and die.

Cathedral Falls wasn't far. In the cold air, the scent of rotting leaves grew strong. The underbrush thickened and the sound of the falls crashed ahead. I finally pushed out of the woods and onto a bank near the base of the waterfall. Water plunged from the rock face above, a thirty-foot drop over craggy ledges to the pool below. Even in my apprehension, I looked up in awe.

I called for Liz again. She couldn't have gone much farther. Just when I thought she must have hurt herself somewhere along the way, I heard a voice from near the waterfall. I stepped closer and searched the bank in the dying light. Spray blew into my already wet face and tracked down the front of my coat. The water and the coming nightfall chilled the air. I called one more time and heard Liz's voice in return, the sound dulled by the rain and the trees. A flash of yellow shirt caught my eye. Fifty feet downstream, nearly obscured from sight by tangled bushes and a bend in the creek, Liz had found the excavation. She knelt at the edge, covered in mud, pushing ooze and branches and dead leaves into the pit.

~

The waning daylight left time only for a cursory look at Bob's excavation. Even though rain and Liz's efforts marred it, the large square had been cut straight into the earth, a few lines of string remained at the edges. The work looked like the dig I'd seen at Lake Ozette, the real thing.

I turned my attention to Liz.

She didn't question my presence—as if mental health professionals hiked in to evaluate people all the time. Her face was pale and transparent. Veins showed in lavender-blue tracings along her jaw. She shook from the cold.

At the hospital, Liz had asked what happened to Alfred Mallecke. Maybe she didn't know he was dead or didn't want to believe it. But I thought she had seen what happened on the banks of the Snoqualmie River. Some people don't remember anything that happened during their psychosis. Some can't organize their thoughts well enough to say, and others just won't tell. Liz started talking and I wondered if I'd find out.

"I walked most of the way into Seattle that day," she said.

"What day?"

"The day I saw you at the Star."

I let her talk to see if more information would follow. At the same time, I put each mud-caked arm into a sleeve of the wool jacket I'd brought from the truck. She leaned on my shoulder while I slid her foot into the shoe.

"My feet were swollen from being pregnant and there were blisters on my heels. I folded the backs of my shoes over and kept going. Finally, some guy gave me a ride. He tried to hit on me, but I told him he was Satan if he touched a pregnant woman, so he left me alone."

She made sense for now, but that didn't mean psychosis wasn't lurking under the surface. When I saw her on the psychiatric unit, she had been coherent until I asked her about Alfred Mallecke. I ached to ask now. I knew I was close to learning what happened to him and to Martin. But light was fading fast and I was afraid that if I asked questions it would be harder, if not impossible, to get Liz off the hillside. I could wait until we were safely back to my truck.

Liz's words rambled.

"They're not going to let me keep this baby," she said, maybe the first time she'd spoken of her pregnancy. "All I can do is pray for the others now. The dead want to be at rest."

Liz did look beatific, like an angel in a red plaid coat. She changed to another subject. "Len and I stopped by his Uncle Felix's house. Everyone sat around the kitchen table. The man with the camera came. Felix talked about this dig." She waved her hand at the straight-edged hole, still marked with string where she hadn't finished covering it. "He said the shaggy guy had done it. The ancestors, he'd disturbed them. I have to pray now."

"Bob?" I handed her the candy bar first, and she took a delicate bite.

Liz didn't answer. "Felix was angry. He told Martin he'd never understand." She pulled the wool jacket tight. "God wanted me to get out of there."

I took her hand and guided her toward the path while she talked.

Liz jerked away. "I'm not finished here."

I put my arm around her shoulder. The little bit of daylight that remained had turned a duskier gray. "Please . . ."

"I've got to put the people to rest. I love Leonard, but he'd never go against his uncle. I've got to set things right with their ancestors."

That belief could harm Liz and her baby. "I'm afraid you really can't set everything right. We've got to get you home."

She gave me an otherworldly smile. "Of course I can't make everything right."

Liz reminded me of the Michelangelo painting at the Sistine Chapel. She held her hand out like a mud-covered Moses touching the hand of God. She was pointing to the dig. "But I'm not leaving until I bury these bones."

Chapter 23

IN THE DIM LIGHT, I saw the outline of the spot where Bob had carefully measured and moved soil, artifacts, and bones. Clots of underbrush ran up to the creek and concealed the excavation. Liz's leaves and mud hid it further, and mats of branches that had covered it lay nearby. I was surprised anyone had found Bob's secret. But the contents of the dig had spread far. Martin had bones; Bob had bones. Now Liz.

"Where did you get those?" I whispered, as if there were anyone to hear. I shined the flashlight on the muddy pit where an armload of the now familiar yellowed remains lay half-covered.

"The van."

Felix had bones.

I didn't interfere with her plan to rebury them. A power struggle would have taken longer than the interment. The dark colors of ground, forest and sky bled into each other. Liz pushed dirt from a collapsed side of the pit until none of the remains were visible. Her task complete, she wiped her hands on the coat and let me lead her away. I kept her in front of me on the trail and trained the flashlight far enough ahead for us both to see.

"The underground people are quieter now," she said.

"Are those the voices you hear?" I asked.

"Yes," Liz slipped on the slick path. Her center of gravity was off. Liz walked with the swaybacked posture of a very pregnant woman. I held her arm to steady her. We gave up talk to concentrate on our feet.

The closer we got to the road, the more I wondered what to do about Liz. I didn't trust her to drive away in Felix's van. She needed to go to the hospital. Her words might have had a kernel of truth, but her behavior was unsafe enough to get her committed. Exposure to Northwest weather at nightfall with no coat and one shoe wasn't great judgment in March, or even in May or June most years.

The problem was, no one else had witnessed Liz's behavior. I was the only one who could write an affidavit to have her hospitalized. That would mean a drive to the hospital or a wait for the MHP on duty to show up. Either option was sure to last most of the evening. The detour to the falls had taken more than an hour already. Frank and Nell would be mad with worry. I had told them I'd be right home.

The path leveled out and widened enough to allow us to walk side by side. We were out of the trees. Full darkness pressed down on ragged fields.

"I'll drive you back to Leonard's house," I told her. "Richard is there. Someone can pick the van up later." As soon as I said it, I worried about Felix.

So did Liz. "No," she said and ran back toward the woods. She didn't mean to stop, but the thin leather soles of her shoes slid out from under her before she'd gone three steps. I caught up when she dropped to her knees.

"Promise you won't make me go," she said and bowed her head to mutter furious prayers.

"Liz..."

"I'll go back to the Star Hotel."

"No." I'd only seen my daughter once in the past three months. I needed to be there. "I don't have time to drive you there—my family is waiting. I won't let you take the van." I wrapped my fingers around the key in my pocket.

"Give me bus fare."

"Leonard helps you. He'll keep you safe." I wanted someone else to get her back to the hospital. I'd reached my limit. Somehow, I got Liz to start walking again. Her steps were stiff and hesitant.

"Safe?" Liz's voice was shrill. "Felix goes there. That's not safe."

That was what I was afraid of. Liz trembled with fear.

"That day we visited Felix," Liz's words ran together, "they sat around the kitchen table, all men. Felix was angry. He argued with that Martin guy—told him he'd never understand, 'White people don't care about their own ancestors,' is what he said."

She kept her distance and muttered to her voices between parts of the story. The water in the wetlands pooled higher and lapped over edges of the trail ahead. The rain had stopped, probably not for long.

"Felix jumped up and said he was going to see Bob. Everybody held him back. You don't want Uncle Felix running out when he's mad. Martin said to let him handle it. Felix went off over that and said he'd handle it himself."

That sounded consistent with what I knew about Felix. "What did he do?"

"I don't know. I left." Liz still stood in the middle of the trail. When she turned toward me, I couldn't see her face for the darkness. But her voice was solemn. "You know how people say, 'I'm going to kill him,' but they really don't mean it. They're just so angry they feel like it. I really thought Felix was going to kill Bob. I know I was getting crazy, but that's what I thought."

She mouthed a few words under her breath before she went on with the story. "When I got back from the hospital yesterday, Felix was pissed off at Bob. And how Bob had said this and done that. I was relieved, that meant Bob was still alive. That was yesterday. Today Richard calls and says that Bob was terribly murdered."

I touched her arm. "Liz, did you see—"

"I'm not family. I'm an outsider," her words rushed on. "Felix will trust Len and Richard to stick by him, but he won't trust me."

I gave up my good intentions about not questioning her until we were back to the truck. She seemed so close to saying something that would answer my questions about whether she had seen Martin or Mallecke die. "Did you see the murders at the river?"

She prayed. "Lord keep me safe. Keep the children safe. Take me somewhere safe. Safe, safe, safe."

"I'll help you," I said, though at the moment I didn't know how. "Did you see the murders?"

It was dark, but I imagined I could see the whites of her eyes.

"Did you go to the river with Alfred Mallecke?"

"Yes." Her voice was a wisp of breath so quiet I wondered if I had heard it. We were close enough to the road for a rumble from a passing truck to shake the ground.

"Tell me."

"I got to Seattle and slept at the Star Hotel. I knew Alf from before."

"Alf." The diminutive of his name was so intimate that a pang of loss swept over me. I thought of his shrunken body at the morgue and felt helpless in the face of it.

"Alfred," Liz went on. "That day he was talking crazier than I was, said he ate a pigeon live. But I didn't believe that. He said things to shock me."

He did those things too, I thought. But Liz was right about the shock effect. Mallecke didn't think the pigeon was a demon; he was looking for a reaction. And got it. That's why I had been called and one reason why I hadn't committed him. But he did have voices and they told him he wasn't safe. Psychotic thoughts could reflect very real feelings and events.

"I didn't have any money. So I asked Alf where he was staying. I knew it would be on the streets, but he was a good person to hang around. Other men wouldn't bother me then." Liz's words came fast and took a turn without warning. She raised her hands to her ears. "I still hear the people underground. I thought they would stop."

I tried to piece her story together with what I knew but got as distracted by her voices as she did. "What are they saying?" I said, but she kept going.

"The underground people say someone's after the homeless people, to beat us and kill us."

That sounded too like Alfred Mallecke's words. "Liz," I said. "What's happening on the streets?"

"Four in the hospital, one man died." She stopped to pray again.

"Keep going," I whispered, meaning both the walking and the story.

"The shelters are full, they turn you away. The workers say the best thing to do is to take a bus away from downtown, sleep in one of the parks where no one would look for a homeless person."

"That's why you and Alfred went to the river."

"I took him there because he helped me and I wanted to take him to a safe place. Oh no, oh god..." Then she stopped and didn't say anything more.

"What happened?" I asked, but she was mute. Liz had hit a wall. She stood in the middle of the muddy trail and seemed unaware of the rain streaming over her face.

"Did you see the murders?"

Liz clutched her belly and shook her head no, then yes, then no. She went back to the chanting like she'd done the first night I saw her. "I've got to save the children. They're charred and marred, like the gas man guard, the gas man burned. The gas man turned. Burn, burn, burn."

I was thankful when she resumed her jerky walk toward the road.

She knew, I thought. She knew what happened to Mallecke. And to Martin.

"You can come home with me," I said and found myself shaking. I told myself it was from the cold, but I was convinced that Liz wasn't safe either. I couldn't let her go like I did Alfred Mallecke.

Liz's voice was sad. "You can't set everything right either."

"No." I felt suddenly hopeless.

Liz gripped my arm—to steady herself, or me. Her arm felt thin but strong through the wool jacket. We walked toward the road with mud sucking at our feet.

"We can drive by Len's house," she said between her prayers. "If Felix isn't back yet, I'll go in. Richard will help me find a place to go."

"The hospital," I suggested, but the chances of that were slim.

~

When we got back to Leonard's house at Kayak Lake, Liz seemed relieved to find out Felix hadn't returned. I helped her change into a pair of long johns and two layers of Leonard's shirts and then sat her in front of the woodstove. Richard wrapped her in a scratchy wool blanket while she rambled about how I'd found her at the falls. I clarified the story before leaving her in Richard's care. When I finally headed out the door, they were debating whether she would go to the hospital.

I arrived home to glowing windows and smoke spiraling from the chimney like a child's idealized drawing. Inside, the air was warm and smelled of marinara sauce and bread. But the welcome was strained. Frank and Nell were frenzied after waiting first one hour and then another. The story I told them didn't help.

"Jesus Christ." Frank's face turned to stone when he was angry. "What were you thinking? You went to see Bob Swan by yourself. Then Felix George. Then the falls. Why?"

"I just went. It made sense at the time."

Nell picked up the torch of reprimanding Mom. "And now we know he threatened Bob Swan. Bob Swan is dead. Martin and the homeless man too. You put yourself out there by asking all these questions. Think about the consequences."

She sounded just like me when I lectured her.

Gwen was already there, wearing a low-cut sweater. She looked pulled together, at least on the surface. She'd handled the memorial all right—up until the scene with Bob. Now, she took over, a role reversal. She marched me upstairs, stripped off my wet clothing and handed me dry jeans and wool socks and sweaters she found in the armoire. I didn't mind being taken care of for once.

The puppy left a trail of mud behind him when he followed me in from the truck. Gwen rubbed him down with an old towel. Caesar followed her eager for more attention.

The bone-deep chill from my evening at the falls wouldn't leave. I wrapped myself in a tightly woven blanket and sat on the raised brick hearth within inches of the wood stove. I built the fire up, but the warmth felt superficial.

Nell's sweet face, heart-shaped and framed by the new hairstyle curving in at the cheek, wore the same stony expression as Frank. She harangued me about dangerous situations. She circled me until I felt crowded and she couldn't let it go. "If you wanted to look in Martin's house, fine. If you wanted to look at the computer disks, fine. But you go off with people you have no reason to trust."

"Look." I threw up my hands. "Nobody was after me. No one tried to hurt me. I'm sorry I made you worry." But I was worried too and more than I was about to admit.

"Nobody fucking tried to hurt you today. But they already broke into the little house—my space." Nell ignored the old rule that kids don't swear around adults and vice-versa. Or maybe she just bumped her way into the adult club. She didn't seem to care.

"What am I supposed to do, wait passively for something else to happen? You can help. Bob's neighbor doesn't speak English. She's a Spanish speaker and she saw something last night. You could translate."

Frank jumped in. "Don't get her involved, Grace."

Nell put her hands on her hips. "But I want to help."

It was perfect. Now she could react against Frank.

After a few more volleys in the argument, Nell and I went to the phone with a common cause. I found the scrap of paper with Clara's number and dialed, but instead of a human voice, an answering machine beeped. I handed the phone to Nell to leave a message.

~

After dinner, we carried the empty plates from the table into the kitchen and opened another bottle of wine. Gwen's low-cut sweater exposed so much skin that I felt cold just looking at her.

"I feel like I made this happen," she said. "I wished Bob Swan was dead. His scheme for Cathedral Falls made me that mad."

"His murder probably will stop the quarry." I poured more wine around.

"All along, I thought that Bob killed Martin." Gwen cradled her head in concentration. "He wasn't antisocial enough to plan it out. I feel so stupid."

I touched Gwen's sleeve. She looked at me with brimming eyes. Before, her reactions had felt wild and on the verge of losing control. Her tears seemed right.

Nell stumbled off to the couch, tired again after her all-night flight. I still thought of her as Nell in private moments. I respected her request to be called Helen—it was a lovely name—after all, Frank and I had chosen it. But a habit that long term was hard to break. Whatever I called her, she dozed off.

Gwen lit a fresh candle to replace the smoldering nub in the Chianti bottle we used for a holder. Drips of old wax ran over the glass in dried rivers of blue, yellow, and green. The new candle was red. The first drip of hot wax rolled onto the lip of the bottle and clung suspended, a growing red bulb ready to burst and slide over the shoulder.

"You're right about Bob," Frank said. "He was not the pre-meditating type." Nell sighed and rolled over on the couch. Frank lowered his voice. "Let's not wake up Nell."

"Helen." I reminded him.

"I remember when you first started calling her Nell," Gwen said. The brittle quality she'd worn ever since Martin's death had softened. "She was about five and always introduced herself as Hellion. I think you guys were afraid she'd do that when she got to grade school."

"Little Hellion wasn't afraid of anything," I glanced over my shoulder to where she slept. "Not the dark, not scary stories, not strangers. When we lived in Seattle, there was a homeless guy who lived in the park behind us. We didn't even know it until Nell came in from the yard with little presents and this new nickname he gave her. She insisted on being called Hellion. We finally figured out she was meeting him over the back fence every day. I couldn't let her play out there alone after that."

"I remember him," came a sleepy voice from the couch. "He was really nice."

"Ever heard about taking candy from strangers?" I asked.

"I was a good judge of character even then."

"You were five."

"Did I really insist on being called that?"

"Yes, my darling Hellion, you did." I might prefer that to Helen now.

Gwen got up and stretched. "I've got to get home."

"One more thing," I said as I helped her gather her things. "How about taking Caesar for a few days. You know, visitation. I can't let the chickens range free while he's here."

Gwen looked down at the pup, who was glued to her knee in adoration. She patted his head in the stiff way of a person who doesn't much care for dogs. "I should be flattered that he loves me. We have to find this guy a real home before he gets too attached."

Caesar bounced down on his front paws, then barked and stared at Gwen. Maybe he was telling her it was too late.

She didn't buy it. "At least he has space to run out here. If you keep him for a few more days, I'll take him on the weekend when I have time to walk him."

I left the dishes in the sink and crawled into bed as soon as Gwen pulled out of the driveway. Frank followed me upstairs. But Nell was stirring again. "Have you watched the cuts from Martin's film yet?" she asked.

Our bedroom was an open loft tucked under the rafters. The fire threw wild shadows on the walls and ceiling. Frank leaned on the railing and shook his head at Nell on the couch below. "His computer was stolen, so there's nothing to look at."

"I'm sure he had everything backed up. Bet I can find his discs." The couch springs creaked and covers rustled as Nell sat up. "I can't get back to sleep. Let's go over and look."

Frank sat down on the bed to pull off his shoes and the springs squeaked. "Not me."

"Not me," I echoed and pulled the covers over my head.

"Tomorrow then." I heard Nell flop back on the couch. In spite of her protest that she was wide awake, the sound of her breathing came slow and heavy as soon as she hit the cushions.

Chapter 24

COLD AIR SEEPED through the blankets. Half asleep, I reached for Frank to warm me, but his side of the bed was empty. The phone rang from far away, but by the time I pulled myself out of my dream, it stopped.

"Grace," Frank whispered from downstairs. "It's Gwen."

"What time is it?" I asked and reached for the alarm before he answered. Eight o'clock. Frank would be on his way to work in a minute and Gwen would already be at school. I threw back the covers and stumbled down to the kitchen where I could talk without waking Nell.

Before I picked up the phone, I poured a cup of coffee and leaned my forehead against the cold window glass—where I'd stood a week ago, watching the chickens. Before Caesar and the rooster. Before Martin. And Alfred Mallecke. And Bob Swan. Beyond the trees, Martin's house stood as an empty reminder of their deaths.

Gwen didn't waste time on small talk. She raised her voice over the slam of locker doors and laughter in the background. "Carl Ring called."

I braced myself for more bad news.

"To give me an update on Martin's murder investigation."

"What?"

"It wasn't only artifacts in the back of Bob's truck. They found Martin's computer too."

And just when our supper table tribunal had cleared him, I thought. An oily smear marred the window where I had rested my forehead. I tried to wipe it away with the hem of my bathrobe, but I only made it worse.

~

Frank was behind schedule at his remodeling job because he had taken yesterday off to pick up Nell. On his way out the door, he said that he'd be working late. I called around to find a replacement for my shift that evening. I wanted to spend time with Nell. Normally, she'd have preferred her friends' company to mine, but their spring break hadn't started yet. She was at loose ends. I also didn't mind acting out a little after my supervisor's reprimand. Or spending the day in what seemed to be a useless search for answers.

Nell wanted to look for the outtakes from Martin's film. She liked playing detective too. We trekked single file through the woods to Martin's. Caesar looped figure eights around us, first running ahead, then behind. The morning paper said we'd had precipitation every day for the last ninety days. The usual puddles along the path had turned to small lakes that were big enough to name.

When we got to the house, Caesar ran under the alders while a squirrel scolded him and jumped from tree to tree in the high branches. My mind stayed tied to recent events. The computer was in Bob's truck, but did the fingerprints in Martin's house belong to him? To Felix? To someone else? A piece was missing. We left the puppy outside and stepped into the cold house.

Nell looked around in silence for a while. "I used to play here under the steps," she finally said and pointed. Her eyes were smudged with dark circles. This was Nell's first time here since Martin's death.

"I'm sorry you missed the memorial," I struggled with an apology. "I wish I hadn't told you to stay in Mexico. But I was so worried and I thought I could protect you as if you were still a kid. You're not."

"It's okay."

"Maybe we can have our own memorial before we look for more discs."

Nell found a candle to light in his memory and made a shrine with a picture and a few things she found outside: a pinecone, a pretty rock, and a bed of moss. Then we had a moment of silence before she headed back towards the door.

"Where are you going?" I asked.

"Martin kept his backup discs in the shed. You know, heating with wood, he was more afraid of losing everything to fire than a computer crash."

I shuddered at the thought of visiting the shed again, but Nell found what she was looking for in a matter of minutes and I rushed her back home through the woods.

In high school, Nell's senior project had been a film about homelessness. She'd loved it when I got her introductions to the shelters in downtown Seattle. I'd loved it when she looked up to me and my expertise. She made a thoughtful film that neither romanticized nor demonized the people she'd met on the street: the Alfred Malleckes, the men living under the freeway like Red, and women like Liz. I had been impressed by Nell's technical skills too. Now she slid Martin's work into the disc drive of my new computer and the screen came to life.

"Martin was my community supervisor for the project. He's the one who taught me." Anger tinged the sadness in her voice. Pictures of old folks' reminiscences rolled by on the screen, the less interesting stories, the shots ruined by mannerisms that distracted.

"He's got a bunch of junk here." Nell swiveled right and left in the office chair. "Filmmakers cut hours and hours for everything that's used."

When Caesar whined at the door, I let him in and grabbed an old towel to wipe him down, but it seemed hopeless. Lydia Taylor had a mudroom that never saw a speck of dirt; we just had the mud. I thought about her out here, away from suburbia where houses were always clean. I pictured her with Martin sitting by his fire, all candlelight and romance. I didn't see her hauling wood, repairing leaks or mucking around with animals. Lydia was a houseguest in this world. She had two sides that were perfectly split by the men she chose. Will for the ambitious Lydia. Martin for the artistic one. Never the twain shall meet.

Caesar curled up at Nell's feet and I watched over her shoulder. She scanned fast through most of the scenes. Finally, she found Cathedral Falls and Felix George and slowed it down.

"Look." Nell slipped a different disc back into the computer to compare pictures. "The season changes. He used mostly moss and ferns for the background, so you can hardly tell." She changed the disc one more time. "This is spring. The shrubs are bare, but if you look closely you can see the leaf buds are just beginning to swell. I don't think the dig was there in these early shots."

In the later shot, the camera showed a brush pile that extended into the creek. Growth from the forest understory twined and tangled with the brush. The scrub growth had nearly hidden it forever. It looked like a beaver dam gone wild. But along one side, the pile had shifted or been moved away. A slice of the muddy dig was visible.

Nell paused the film. The chair squeaked as she leaned back. "Bob dug after the first time they filmed. Maybe if you watched the finished film closely, you'd see enough to get a hint of the dig, but I doubt it. Martin edited it out. But Bob didn't know that. He must have been afraid it would expose him, so he tried to get rid of the evidence—but the computer and disc weren't his problem. He didn't find this."

Nell was right. Bob had a clear reason for wanting the film, but he had more to worry about.

She hit play again. Felix walked into the shot and began moving debris. Branches cracked as he dragged them away. Martin must have moved in closer with the camera. Brush filled the screen. He didn't seem to be aiming as he shot. Then he spoke, "Pull more aside so we can see what we've got here."

Hearing Martin's voice shocked us, like a ghost. Caesar cocked his head. Unconsciously, Nell and I both looked around the room as if we'd find him there. The picture jerked up on the monitor. Felix shucked away woody growth. Then Felix's voice. "Bob Swan had an interest in archaeology. I'm thinking he plundered some graves here." The camera focused on the ground. We heard, but couldn't see, more brush being moved. Felix's voice again, perhaps unaware the camera was running. "He won't get away with this."

Nell and I looked at each other and let the rest of the pictures spin by unwatched.

~

"So you trust this law student, Richard Black," Nell asked after we'd watched the scene half a dozen more times. We stepped outside for a breather and tossed a stick for the puppy. Caesar bounded through the tall grass like a wind-up toy.

"Yeah, I think Richard's a good kid. He's really into the tribe and seems to care about people."

"What about Felix?" she asked. "Do you trust him?"

The sky was still a uniform gray, darker when we entered the woods between our houses. "I don't know. There seems to be some evidence stacking up against him. But it's not even that I don't trust him. He doesn't trust me—or maybe anybody. Do I think he threatens people? Yes. Do I think he lies? Maybe." The underlying question, of course, was did I think he killed. I didn't have the answer to that.

"From what you tell me, Liz sure doesn't trust him and she's been around him more than you have."

"Yep," I said. "She's super sensitive and her gut feelings are either right on or distorted to hell."

"We'll probably never know." Nell turned her attention back to the puppy. "Let's teach Caesar to play hide and seek."

I held him by the collar while Nell hid behind a tree. As soon as I let him go, he sniffed for her trail and found her. Caesar was better at hide and seek than I was. Just when I thought he had a real skill, he found another squirrel to chase and took off down the muddy path around the pond, leaving Nell waiting to be found.

Heavy drops of rain began to splatter on our faces, signaling that it was time to go in. I followed Nell into the house and put the old towel by the back door to wipe Caesar down again when he came in. Then Nell turned back and surprised me with a hug.

"Thanks for your help," I told her and planted a kiss on her forehead.

She looked as if she wanted to tell me something. Finally, she said, "You know, you don't look like you're ever afraid either," referring to our conversation about her Hellion days the previous evening.

I waited for her to go on.

"Are you?" she asked. "Are you ever afraid at work? Or now, with the murders?"

"Sometimes I'm terrified."

My job carried a risk of being hurt. But worse than that was my fear of making a decision that caused someone else hurt. I thought back to the day I talked to Red under the freeway. He told me I wasn't that big. Not big enough to protect all the troubled people I wanted to help. "I guess I try not to show it when I'm afraid. What about you?"

"I get scared. But it's like I get fascinated too, especially when I'm scared. Like with that homeless guy when we lived in Seattle. One time he did try to grab me."

"Oh God," I said. "Now you tell me."

"I jumped back and told him off and he never tried it again. I knew he wouldn't."

I could picture five-year-old Nell fending him off with the intensity that showed on her face now.

"But I still knew he was kind of dangerous. When I get scared, I like knowing I can handle it."

"You're tough, girl." I squeezed her hand. "But you don't have to be tough all the time."

"Why not? You are." She challenged me with her smile.

I smiled back and wished I spawned a daughter who was a little more circumspect.

We stood at the refrigerator and picked at leftovers with our fingers.

I thought about being afraid, the shudder I still felt when I thought of Nell's little house by the pond and the break-in. We would all be afraid until the killer was caught. But I didn't have to be passive. "Okay, Miss Helen. Let's make a hot dish to take to Mr. Swan for condolences. And let's ask him some questions. I dug through the refrigerator with more purpose.

"Questions about what?"

"Bob."

Helen grated cheese while I boiled the noodles. We were arranging a container of pasta in a basket when the phone rang.

It was Richard Black with an update. In an unhurried way, he told me he had talked to Carl Ring about the bones at Martin's house and in Bob's truck. The police had not notified the tribe about either. Carl had been polite but not forthcoming. He said all bones had to be seen by the medical examiner—that's how they knew whether to contact the tribe or open another murder investigation. He asked Richard to be patient. Richard said he might be more patient if Carl kept him informed.

I finally asked what I really wanted to know. "What happened with Liz?"

"Good news. She agreed to go to the hospital. She signed in as a voluntary patient on the eastside."

"That's great. My daughter and I were just on our way out. Maybe we'll stop by and visit." Bob's father was in Woodinville. From there, the hospital was just a few miles south on 405.

"You're going out?" Richard asked. "I thought you were expecting Felix."

I felt that shudder of fear again, the hairs on my neck standing up. "What do you mean?"

"That's why I called. Felix said you left a note for him at the tribal center—that you wanted him to come up to your house and talk. I figured it was about Bob Swan and the bones."

The phone slipped from my ear. I caught it and straightened up. "Felix might have said he was coming, but I did not leave a note."

Chapter 25

"I'VE GOT TO FIND A COAT," Nell said when I told her I wanted to leave right away. Her cold weather clothing had been pushed to the back of the closet while she was in Mexico.

I grabbed one of Frank's heavy jackets and handed it to her. With every wasted second, I saw more danger. There was no way to know if Felix was lying about getting a message or if someone had actually left it. I just had a very bad feeling.

"If he'd called me, I could have arranged to meet him in a public place just to be careful." I grabbed the picnic basket for Mr. Swan, put my free hand on Nell's shoulder and turned her toward the front door. "We're alone and far from town."

I looked around to make sure we had everything and grabbed Martin's backup discs to take to the police station.

"I'll call the puppy," Nell said. On the porch, she whistled for Caesar, but he hadn't returned from his romp with the squirrel. She started around the house to look for him, but I rushed her to the truck instead.

"I don't think we should wait." Maybe Nell wanted to flirt with danger. Maybe at twenty, she didn't have the full concept of which situations to avoid.

I didn't know if I should feel threatened by Felix, but Liz did. She'd never said that he had made the threatening phone call to the hospital. But I'd seen enough on the film to make me wonder about Bob's murder. And Felix had spent time in prison for killing a man. I knew that the biggest predictor of violence in the future is a history of violent acts in the past. Maybe Richard had been mistaken about Felix having a note from me.

But if Felix had my address, I wanted to know why. I wasn't in the phone book.

After two tries, I got the key in the ignition. My hand shook, but it was barely perceptible. On the way down the hill into town, I feathered the brakes going into the curves and accelerated on the way out. We bounced over the bumps on the truck's stiff suspension. So far, we hadn't passed the blue, pinstriped van.

"You're moving fast, Mom. You look a little nervous."

"And you're just fascinated to see what happens next." I glanced away from the road. Nell sat straight on the seat next to me, her face bright. "I'll tell you something about being scared. It's good information. I'd rather listen to my fear than be complacent. The worst that can happen then is I get embarrassed for being wrong."

"By the way, how long are you planning to stay away from the house? If Felix is such a bad guy, he could just wait there until we got back."

"I don't know. Let's drop the casserole off at Mr. Swan's and figure out what to do from there."

Nell curled her lip in a sneer at the basket wedged between us on the seat. "Mr. Swan is a drag. Can I wait in the car while you take it in?"

"No."

"Well, we should check in with Carl Ring at the police station first. And what about Bob's neighbor at the trailer park—you still want me to interpret?"

"Okay. We'll do the police before Mr. Swan and the neighbor after."

Nell loved to use logic to get what she wanted—at the moment that was to avoid the condolence thing. But she was right. I wanted to talk to Clara and I needed to go to the police. I had a little information and a lot of concerns to discuss with Carl Ring. So when I got to the valley, I passed up the bridge to Woodinville and drove along the swollen river into town and the police station. But the only person at the station was the receptionist behind her Plexiglas. Nell and I left the discs and a detailed note for Carl Ring at the desk. Before I left, I called the answering machine and left a message for Frank to tell him not to come home either. I hoped he would call in to check the messages.

~

The Eastside phone book listed Lewis Swan's address in Woodinville. The house was just off Avondale, a four lane arterial that had once been a country road. His Northwest contemporary nestled at the end of a lane. Mature plantings of dogwood, early blooming azaleas and hillocks of ferns and heather connected the rolling lawn to the forest behind. Rain muted the colors. I had talked with Mr. Swan at community functions over the years. Last summer, I ran into father and son at a chamber music festival. Lewis Swan's demeanor was stern and impatient when he was with Bob, unlike the smooth humor he projected at the quarry meeting.

There were no cars in the driveway when we pulled in. No tangle of supportive family and friends had flocked here to comfort Mr. Swan. His wife had died of cancer a few years ago, so he could use the dinner we'd packed. If he was home, his car was in the garage.

Nell and I raced to the door through the rain. Wind sprayed water onto the covered entry. Finally, I heard footsteps. Mr. Swan wasn't the sort of man you'd call by his first name. His demeanor demanded respect. The door opened.

"Mr. Swan." The right words don't exist for losing a son to murder. "I stopped by to tell you how sorry I am about Bob. My daughter, Helen, and I brought a dinner for you, so you don't have to worry about cooking."

Nell held out the basket with suitable seriousness.

I could tell he didn't want to invite us in, but he glanced at Nell's offering and inched the door open. "Thank you." He took the food and led us into the house.

A long counter crowded with folders, neat stacks of paper, and a portable television tuned to the stock reports, separated the kitchen from the den. Mr. Swan wore the requisite Northwest flannel shirt with corduroy pants perfectly creased from ironing. No expression showed on his face. He set the basket down near the sink and seemed stuck there for a moment with his arms limp at his sides. Finally, he waved us toward the sitting area. "The police told me that you found him. Bob always had problems, but I never imagined this."

The furniture in the den was arranged at right angles and the end tables were clear of bric-a-brac. No family photos, no little treasures received as gifts over the years and kept on display out of loyalty. I imagined all signs of his wife had been cleared away since her death. He'd have a different kind of cleaning up to do after Bob.

Mr. Swan lowered himself into the easy chair, but stayed at the edge of the seat, rigid and stiff-backed. Nell and I took the couch. Mr. Swan waved again and made a couple nervous chops in the air. "They said he is a suspect in the murder of Martin Hanish. They questioned me about Bob, what I knew about his actions."

"I'm sorry. That doesn't make this any easier." I went light on the sympathy. A lot of men his age were stoic and wouldn't go for it.

"If my son killed that man, he got the consequences he deserved." Mr. Swan talked as if Bob was a kid who had wrecked the car out of carelessness and needed to be taught a lesson in responsibility. Bob had said that he and his father hadn't agreed on anything in decades. Mr. Swan wasn't giving him a break even in death.

"Bob never seemed to find his place in the world," I said. "He had high hopes for the quarry, though. He told me the project brought the two of you together."

Nell sat beside me on the couch, the polite smile frozen on her face.

The corners of Mr. Swan's mouth turned down in a tight-lipped way that seemed habitual. "Bob wasn't happy about it, but that gravel pit idea was on the way to the rubbish bin anyway."

"Really?" I asked. "Did something come out of the public hearing that changed your mind?"

"No." He gave a derisive laugh. I didn't think he considered the community a worthy adversary. "I'm getting old. I couldn't run an operation like that now. I wanted to see Bob have a chance." He stopped and looked down. His pale hands were freckled with liver spots. He ran a thumb over the papery skin on his wrist where a scrape had scabbed over. "Maybe you've heard that Bob dug up some Indian graves. I just found out myself a few days ago. How can Bob run a business when he does things like that? First he thought he'd hide the graves so he wouldn't have to deal with the tribe. Then he dug the mess up and tried to sell it for a fast buck on the Internet. By the time I found out what had happened, the damage was done. Could I go ahead with the quarry after that?"

Mr. Swan sounded human for a moment. But it didn't last any longer than the pause after his rhetorical question—which he answered himself. "I got a much better proposal to develop the property up at Cathedral Falls. When we were working on the permits for the quarry, our environmental specialist came to me with a slick idea."

"Housing development?" I asked.

"That land isn't fit for housing. No, the Lyster Oil Company wants to lease the land for the new Cascade Pipeline."

I looked at Mr. Swan's feet to calm myself. I pictured the wall of flame the TV news had shown coming down the creek when the other pipeline exploded. Liz's ramblings had incorporated it. I stared so hard at Mr. Swan's shoes, that for a minute, I thought they had caught fire.

"That's the pipeline they wanted to build in North Bend. You're talking about moving it to Duvall? After the explosion and the boys who died?"

"The oil lease appeals to me. Good income, right? Half of the permits we need for the oil have been done already for the quarry. My environmental man is after me to keep going, but I'll probably have to sit back for a while. Let everything cool off, the burial ground, the explosion, the murders."

He looked too cool. One of those murders had been his son, but maybe Mr. Swan had written Bob off so long ago that it hardly felt like a loss.

Nell squirmed beside me on the sofa. "People won't accept a pipeline here."

He dismissed her with a hiss of air that he blew out between his lips. "Not in my backyard, that's everyone's argument. But Americans like their gasoline, and companies are going to move it to them. The plan to locate in North Bend failed because there was big money to fight it there. Weyerhaeuser is building hundreds of luxury homes. They don't want a pipeline to scare off buyers. With their staff of lawyers, Weyerhaeuser made it too costly for Lyster to pursue."

He looked like he was enjoying himself. "Duvall, on the other hand, would be lucky to raise enough money to hire a lawyer for a few hours a month. We could run their bank account to zero in no time. My show would go on."

People responded to stress in a lot of different ways. Most of us just did our usual thing but more of it. If you were compulsive, you got more compulsive. If you were a man who organized his entire life around business, you went on with your business.

Something about what Mr. Swan said piqued my interest, but I couldn't pin it down. The connection finally clicked. "Will Taylor," I said.

"Pardon me?"

"Will Taylor. He's your environmental specialist."

"Yes, he is. He used to work for Lyster. That's how he put the plan together."

Nell rearranged herself on the seat next to me. I reached over to squeeze her hand while I thought. "What does he stand to gain?" I asked.

"He bills me by the hour, but I suspect he has something going with Lyster too. Otherwise, he wouldn't mind the wait while all the mess around the property settles."

"He's in a hurry," I said, remembering what Lydia had said about their financial problems.

"I'm old enough to wait, but Will is ambitious. Bob couldn't stand him. He thought Will was taking over, with the business plan, with his relationship to me. And I'll admit, Will would have been a more fitting son to me. We think alike."

When I looked at Mr. Swan, I felt like crying. Not so much for his loss of a son but for Bob's loss of a father. I realized I was still clutching Nell's hand. I let go and gave her a pat. Finding the right words to excuse myself was a problem, Mr. Swan wasn't interested in condolences.

Finally, all I could think of to say was "Helen and I don't want to keep you any longer."

We made a dash for the car. The information about the pipeline raised one new question. When Liz was at her most psychotic, she talked about the gas man.

Chapter 26

THE WINDSHIELD WIPERS slapped at the rain and smeared arcs of water in their path. I turned east and pointed toward home. But Nell and I couldn't go all the way home until we knew for sure we would not meet Felix George there.

"Didn't Mr. Swan ever love his son?" Nell asked.

"Not recently, I guess. He's got a replacement all picked out in Lydia's husband, though. It's sad. I talked to Will Taylor at the memorial. He had such bad feelings about his own father that he didn't even go to his funeral when he died."

Bare trees made a tunnel on Woodinville-Duvall Road, branches touching branches over the road. Moss grew thick on the old maples, the bark obscured by the mottled coat. The road cut a straight swath through the primordial green. The mood and the rain lightened when we reached the valley. Back in Duvall, Nell and I would pry deeper into the life of Bob—the bad son. I hoped Clara, his Spanish-speaking neighbor, was home now that I had Nell to interpret.

I pulled up in front of Bob's trailer. Except for the motorcycle parts, it was tidy enough to be in any middle-class neighborhood. Next door, Clara struggled down the steps with a plastic tricycle under one arm and a jumble of smaller toys in the other. She pulled open the door of a tiny Chevy Geo and tried to stuff them all inside at once. She ended up with a pile of toys in the mud.

Nell and I called to her, but Clara got the car loaded, mud and all, hurried back to her trailer and shut the door without acknowledging us.

"She's the same person who plied you with coffee yesterday?" Nell asked. "She's not your friend today."

"Let's try anyway," I knocked on the door that closed in our faces.

I heard movement and the little girl's voice inside, but the door didn't budge.

Nell took over. She knocked again and spoke to the door in Spanish. When Clara still didn't answer, Nell leaned her cheek against the door and began a calm and steady stream of words. The reassuring sound of her voice worked: Clara's door swung open.

Nell and I stepped inside to a room scattered with half-filled suitcases. Nell spoke to Clara in rapid Spanish and didn't bother to include me. The conversation was too fast for me to follow. Nell knew what to ask; she could do the translation later.

Clara filled a suitcase with tiny ruffled dresses while she spoke. The little girl frowned with concentration and pulled each dress out again as soon as it was packed away. Clara reprimanded her in a shrill voice. I knelt down to distract the girl with a picture book I found on the couch. When I opened the book, an electronic "baa" came out of the mouth of a woolly sheep. Then Clara's daughter reached to turn the page and show me what happened next.

Clara closed the overstuffed suitcase and began to fill another. Nell came down to the floor where the toddler and I now sat cross-legged. "She says the police were here about an hour ago. They didn't speak Spanish, but they talked to her in English real loud. Clara was afraid they'd ask about her documentation and wouldn't let them in. Finally, one of them held up a cell phone. They had an interpreter on the line. Then they asked her a bunch of questions about Bob."

"What?"

"They wanted to know his comings and goings. She wasn't much help on that—except for the night he was murdered."

Clara ran out of suitcases and started on cardboard boxes. She rolled up her shirtsleeves and pushed back wisps of hair that had escaped her no-nonsense ponytail. In contrast to Mr. Swan's house, Clara's space was crowded with family photographs. She piled them into a carton to take with her. I had never packed that fast.

Nell jumped up to carry a box to the door. "Here's what she told me."

I smiled at the authority in her voice.

"Clara heard loud voices coming from Bob's trailer at about 7:00 that evening. She ignored them at first, but when they got louder, she looked out. Bob stood in his front door. The other guy was on the steps like Bob wouldn't let him in. She didn't understand anything they said, but there was a lot of hand waving and angry words."

I looked over at Clara. Now she was perched on the edge of the couch like a bird about to flit away. Her daughter held the farm animal book up. It said, "Moo." Boxes and suitcases were lined up at the door.

"What did he look like?"

"Easy to describe. He had a big mole on his cheek and short, gray hair that stood straight up, dark skin."

"We know who that is." I pictured Felix George and Bob under the porch light. They had something to argue about: the bag of bones and artifacts in Bob's truck.

Clara didn't last long on the couch. She sprsng up and fired away in Spanish, worry in her voice. She was probably the same age as Nell and I imagined them together under different circumstances. But for now, Clara scribbled a phone number on a slip of paper that she thrust into Nell's hand. Nell put it in her coat and reached for a suitcase. It was time to load the car. I picked up two bags while Clara ushered her daughter out. She managed to fit everything inside the little hatchback.

Nell waved when Clara pulled away. "She's afraid the police will come back with immigration officials, so she's going to stay with a cousin somewhere in Eastern Washington."

"Do you think the police are really interested in her immigration papers?" I asked.

"I doubt it, but she wasn't about to hang around to find out."

I understood her precautions.

Clara's car disappeared around the corner. Nell squinted in frustration. "No one feels safe. God. I can't believe that stuff Mr. Swan said about a pipeline here in town. We should all be afraid of him. What happened with that explosion?"

"It was about a week before you came home." I described how I had gone to the Star Hotel to evaluate Liz and heard about the pipeline fiasco, first from Liz's psychotic statements, then from the news. I told her about the boys' deaths.

"What a horrible way to die," she said.

We climbed into the truck, but I sat there without starting the engine. "The story got to me. It reminded me of when I was a kid and your grandmother was so depressed. When the gas stove blew up."

"I remember hearing about that," Nell said. "When grandma got those big scars on her hand."

"It was about this time of year. Your grandmother hadn't gotten out of bed for a week, not to do laundry, not to cook. Every night, I poured myself a bowl of Rice Krispies for dinner. Those Snap, Crackle, and Pop guys on the box with their chef's hats looked so happy. I felt so lonely. That night, I decided I would cook."

I thought back to the day. The house was so silent that the tick of the clock pounded in my head. My mother lay curled in bed, face to the wall. The blue cabbage roses on her nightdress contrasted with the white sheets and her white skin. Her hair floated over the pillow like a cloud. When she turned over to talk to me, long pauses punctuated her words—as if each sentence came from far away. Her frailty made me want to cry.

I had just turned seven and wanted to please her. I found the foil-covered TV dinners in the freezer and knelt in front of the round-shouldered stove. I turned the knob and pulled open the bottom like I had seen my mother do. The gas jets hissed. The smell of rotten eggs collected in the kitchen.

I clasped the paper matches until they were bent and damp in my clumsy hands. I struck match after match without as much as a spark of sulfur. Maybe my mother smelled the gas or heard me muttering over my failure. The shuffling sound of her slippers started from the back bedroom. But she didn't move fast. She never moved fast. When she finally reached the kitchen, she wore the bathrobe that matched her gown, blowzy with overblown roses. She knelt down by me.

The last match caught. I flung it into the broiler pan—just as she reached out to grab it. Blue flame exploded from the oven with a boom like thunder and threw me back to the cupboards where the metal handle cut into my shoulder. My mother's loose sleeve caught fire. She screamed. I threw myself on her and she fell back. I pressed into her out of fear. The ends of my pigtails and my sweater curled away from the flame. The sting on my chest seemed to fuse us. Then the fire was smothered between us, leaving the black smell of burnt hair and flesh. It was over.

But something changed. She iced our burns and then took care of me. Wiped my face with a cool cloth. Drove to the store and bought food for the first time in days. My mother sang while she cooked. I had the magical idea that the burn had cured her depression—I thought I saved her.

The cure didn't last. But for years afterward, I would lie in bed at night and make up stories. In every story I was the heroine. First I saved my mother. Then she would sing and make me dinner. And then she told me that she loved me.

~

My fingers were cold on the steering wheel, and our breath fogged the windows in the tiny cab of the truck. Winter rain poured down outside, and Nell looked straight ahead at the steamed glass.

"Why don't you start the car and turn on the defrost?" Nell said and wiped at the windshield after I'd finished. She fingered a split seam on her coat and seemed a bit overwhelmed by the story.

I followed her advice and pulled out of the trailer court, driving on autopilot. The intersection to the highway was on a rise with a view back to the river. The Snoqualmie was full to overflowing and pushed above its banks.

"You never told me that part of the story." Nell said. "How badly were you burned?"

"I was more afraid than hurt."

Nell touched the faint scar at my hairline, one that I usually managed to keep hidden with a wisp of bangs. "That's where this came from?"

I nodded.

She pulled her hand away and wriggled in her seat. I knew she was about to divert me from the serious mood that had settled over the car. "I guess you haven't changed much."

"Meaning?"

"You're still rushing into flames and saving young mothers from their psyches."

I glanced at my sweet-faced daughter wrapped in her father's overcoat.

"Climbing up to Cathedral Falls last night after that pregnant psych patient," she prompted me.

"I'm a glutton for punishment," I said. "But since we're on the subject, I said I'd go visit Liz in the hospital."

Nell rolled her eyes. "It figures. We have to drive all the way back to Bellevue?"

Cars whizzed by on the road and I let the truck idle. "Sorry. But we're not going home." I finally overcame my inertia and made it on to Main Street. What I really wanted was reassurance that it was safe to go home. I checked back at the police station. No Carl. So we headed to see Liz at the hospital. When we arrived, Nell came inside with me to find a warmer, drier place to wait than the truck. I went to see Liz on my own.

On the psychiatric unit, I found Liz in the sterile-looking lounge. She sat with Leonard at a round table by a window with a view of the freeway. Physically, she was healthy enough for the glow of her pregnancy to shine through. But, even from

across the room, the pressure behind her speech and movements was clear. Liz bent forward and talked into Leonard's
face. He avoided her eyes and picked at the edge of the table.
When I joined them, she turned the stream of words toward
me, the same conversation we'd had at Cathedral Falls. Liz
thought Felix was dangerous.

Leonard put his hand on her arm to stop her. "I should
probably tell you. The police have picked up Felix and taken him
into custody. He told me that the fingerprints the police found at
Martin's house belonged to him."

Liz bowed her head and prayed, her words quiet but fast.

"What happened? When?" I questioned Leonard. If the police
had Felix, he was no longer on his way to my house. Maybe that
was why I couldn't find Carl Ring. I could go home.

"Richard called me a few minutes ago. They're questioning
Felix about the murders."

We all sat quietly for a few moments, even Liz. "All the
murders?" I asked. Bob's role still wasn't clear: bones, computer,
houses broken into.

"I don't know. Richard is on his way there to help Felix,"
Leonard said.

"No, no, no," Liz rocked back and forth and crossed herself.

I touched her wrist to steady her but didn't want to wait any
longer to hear what Liz knew. "What did you see at the river,
Liz?"

She bucked back in her chair like I'd hit her.

A nurse wearing a pair of black Levi's with a hospital ID
clipped to the belt came over to the table. I was afraid she was
going to kick me off the unit for upsetting the patient, but she
said, "Are you Grace Vaccaro?"

I looked from her to Liz rocking herself, and back to the
nurse. "Yes."

"Your daughter would like to speak to you. She's waiting
outside."

I put my palms on the table to push myself up. "I'll be right
back."

Liz stood up with me. "Bring her in."

"Your privacy."

"How private are the streets?"

"It's up to you."

The nurse got Nell and pointed her to our table. She made shy eye contact with Liz as I did the introductions, but she didn't sit down. She put her hand on the back of my chair and leaned over me. Her breath carried a hint of chocolate.

"Sorry to bother you, but I got to thinking. Mr. Swan is creepy, betraying his son like that. But this Will guy is the one you shouldn't trust. He conspired against Bob about the gas pipeline. He kept it all a secret."

Liz didn't take her eyes off Nell. "Who?"

Nell glanced to me. "What's his name, Mom?"

"Will Taylor," I said. "He's married to the county council woman."

Nell got over her shyness fast. She talked to Liz matter-of-factly. "He made a deal with Mr. Swan to push through an oil pipeline instead of the gravel pit."

"Him," Liz hissed. "Dark hair and fair skin. Green eyes that burn. He poisons the earth. He burned the children."

"You know about Will and the pipeline?" Nell and I said at the same time.

"The river. Before. Last week. Before." She had the terrified look again. "The dead."

I took a deep breath and tried to slow down because I saw Liz tensing. "I'm trying to understand what you're telling us. Did you see Will at the river?"

Liz froze, but repeated, "The dead." Her voice was filled with terror. The nurse hurried back and directed Liz away from the table, away from us. She walked her back to her room. And then she asked us to leave.

Chapter 27

LIZ'S WORDS placed Will Taylor at the river too. But I wasn't sure when. Will wanted his pipeline. How big an interference had Bob been? Or Martin? My ideas swerved from one man to another. Suspicion was building against Will Taylor, as well as Felix George. But for now we were going home. Felix George was in custody, not a current worry.

When we pulled up the driveway, Caesar lolled on the front porch, back from his romp. But, being home didn't feel idyllic. An aura of foreboding infused the air around us. The sky was leaden and fat drops of water splattered from the eaves, the tree branches, and the electric line that drooped from the pole at the road. A red-tailed hawk cried from the woods, the lonely sound of a hunter.

Inside, Nell curled up on the couch again, still fatigued from her flight. The puppy snuck onto the couch at her feet. I busied myself with chores but couldn't ease the strain.

I thought I would feel safer with Felix in custody, but he seemed to be just one danger.

I wanted Frank here with us, not because he was a man— that hadn't helped Martin or Bob—but because I wanted us all to be together. I listened to the messages on the answering machine. Frank hadn't called home. Instead, there were three messages from Lydia. The anxiety in her voice increased with each call, but she didn't say why she was calling.

I wondered how much she knew about her husband's bait and switch job at Cathedral Falls and his cozy relationship with

Mr. Swan. I wanted to talk to Lydia, all right. But first, I wanted to talk to Carl Ring. He was finally in.

"You picked up Felix George." I said.

"Yes," Carl sounded perturbed.

"Did you read the message I left you? He lied about having a note from me. I was afraid to come home."

"We brought Felix in for questioning. The Mexican girl's statement and the DVDs make him a person of interest. It took most of the day to get an attorney out here so he'd talk to us. If it checks out, he has a good alibi for the night Martin was killed." His speech was oddly formal.

"I heard his fingerprints were all over Martin's house."

"He says he was looking for that box of bones, that he was in Martin's house after it was broken into and saw the same mess you did, but didn't report it—and that's why his fingerprints were there."

"But we know he was at Bob's."

"We do."

Carl's vague answers frustrated me. But as long as I was assured that Felix George wasn't going to show up at my doorstep, I was willing to let it slide. "At least he's being held for now. Is there bail?"

"There wasn't enough evidence to charge him." Carl's voice sounded more realistic. "He left here a few minutes ago."

"Damn it, Carl. Where was he going?"

"Listen, I know you're worried . . . "

"I'll call you later," I said and hung up.

I didn't want to spend time on platitudes. The justification I'd had for coming home was lost. I should have listened to my gut when I got home—I didn't feel right. Now Nell and I would leave again, go up to Lake Joy where Frank would be packing up for the day. It was almost dinnertime. Outside, the day turned to dusk. I hadn't seen the sun all day, but somewhere behind the clouds, it was going down.

The phone rang in my hand as soon as I pushed the off button. I shook Nell awake at the same time I answered it. I wanted her to see my urgency and whispered, "Hurry, we're going to meet your dad," before I said hello.

It was Lydia, her voice tight.

"I can't talk right now," I told her. "I'll call you back."

But council member Lydia wasn't used to being put off. "Give me a minute, I'm worried about Will. You'll know what to do."

Great, I thought, Lydia wants free counseling.

She continued before I could cut her off.

"I opened the mail today. There was a notice of foreclosure on our house. No, that's not where I want to start." She stammered in frustration. "Will confronted me last night about the affair. He knew all along that I was seeing Martin."

"Lydia—" I tried to interrupt.

"I couldn't sleep all night. After I found out about the house, he was pacing and talking crazy, said the pipeline had to pay off because he can't take it anymore."

"How crazy?" I asked. She was worrying me.

Nell wrapped a quilt around her shoulders and listened from the couch. I pointed to her shoes where she'd kicked them off. If she didn't get moving, she'd hold us up too.

"Just now, Will said that everything he'd created was slipping through his fingers. He talked as if I were something he'd created, like Pygmalion."

I wondered if Lydia had begun to suspect her husband of murder. The gas man. In all her fearful ramblings, Liz always came back to the gas man. Will Taylor was the gas man.

Lydia jumped topics. "Will handles the bills. He never told me, but he hadn't paid the mortgage in months. I found out he's hardly had work since December. Every day he dresses up and leaves as if he's going out on a job." Her voice hushed. "But he didn't have any jobs."

I signaled to Nell that we were leaving again. She finally pulled on her shoes. Caesar cocked his head, ready for anything. I told Lydia I would call her back in half an hour and hoped that a concrete time would help. But she was in a panic.

"Listen to me. He heard me leave the last message. He made me tell him that you know about me and Martin too. He was in a rage. I'd never seen him like that. Will is focused on you. He got in his car and drove away."

"He's coming here?" I asked, but I already knew.

"He got deadly calm before he left."

Her choice of words let me know that she did suspect him. I hung up on her. She'd wasted enough of my time. I'd have been gone by now if it hadn't been for Lydia's warning.

~

Daylight was gone. One pair of headlights moved up the road, as someone slowed to find the turnoff in the dark. Tires crunched on the gravel at the bottom of the driveway. Now it was too late. Nell and I had missed our chance to get away.

I tried to make a coherent plan. If we ran through the woods, noise would give us away, especially with the puppy. But if I left Caesar in the house and Will Taylor let him out, Caesar would chase after us and show him our trail. I regretted the time we'd spent teaching him to play hide and seek.

I handed Nell her overcoat and spoke quietly. "You go out the back door. I'll keep the dog back so he doesn't give you away. Get help. Run through the woods to Warshall's. If they're not home, keep going until you find someone who is. And don't come home. I mean it."

Nell amazed me and didn't argue. She looked straight into my eyes and nodded. Little curls from the new haircut clung to her forehead. I wanted to smooth them, but she turned and ran like I told her to.

"Don't let the screen door slam behind you, honey." I called to her back. The reminder sounded fussy and normal, but I wanted her to slip out unheard. Tires spun on gravel, then lights shot up the drive. A moment later, a car pulled up to the front door. I thought of the rooster, who protected the hens by taking on the danger himself. He had led Caesar into the brambles. I hoped I'd come up with an idea half as good.

Chapter 28

A DARK SEDAN pulled into the circle of porch light. I glanced down at the phone still clutched in my hand and punched in 911. I didn't know what to tell the dispatcher. My name and address and "someone is trying to get into my house" seemed to be like a reasonable stretch of the truth that would get a quick response. I could see the driver through the glass. Dark hair, fair skin. Will Taylor. I patted my jeans pocket and found the lump of keys to my truck. Just in case I got to use them.

A gust of wind sent dead leaves flying and made the trees groan. I was glad; the noise would cover any that Nell made as she ran. I pushed Caesar back and stepped out, then shut the door behind me. I decided to meet my fate.

Will pulled himself out of the car and came onto the stone walk just outside the reach of the light.

"Hello, Will." The moment I saw him, I knew that Will was the killer and I was next.

"What a lovely setting you have here." Will indicated my lifeless gardens, brown stalks flattened by months of rain. Any sign of spring was obscured in the darkness. "Lewis Swan told me you had visited to offer sympathy. How kind of you. Thought I'd stop by."

Nobody but a neighbor 'stops by' my house. I live too far from town. I'd thought the same when I heard that Felix George was coming. But I was wrong then. Felix was not the danger. Will's greeting was contrived. He was like a cat toying with his prey, but I was happy to stall for time. I conjured up an illusion of safety and acted calm. He would sense fear.

"Aren't you going to invite me in?" He motioned toward the door. He radiated a dark charm. I remembered his flirtations at the memorial and felt sick.

"We'll have to make it another time." I stepped off the porch to skirt around him. "I'm expected at a friend's house."

Will moved in front of me. "I won't take much of your time."

I judged the distance to my truck, twenty feet on our double gravel driveway, his car in between. A wild dash wouldn't work. He'd be fast enough to grab me. I would have to talk my way out of this.

"You frighten me, Will, I don't feel comfortable inviting you in." I'd learned this on the job, when people sensed unspoken fear they were likely to become threatening. But if I told them I was afraid, I gained their respect. I wanted to be firm, but sympathetic. I wanted to stay in control.

"What?" Will had been too close. He pulled back, a little.

"Lydia just called. You've been having a hard time lately. Your house is being foreclosed. You've had trouble finding work. Your wife was having an affair. That's a lot for a person to handle."

"You don't invite people with problems into your house?" A mild sarcasm tinged his voice. Hostile.

I leaned against the post at the corner of the porch and reminded myself to breathe. The wind flattened Will's coat against his body. With his fists jammed into the pockets, the shape of the raincoat was distorted into a Dali-esque form. The parka was made for mountain wear. I recognized the blue fabric we had found on the rose bush the night of the burglary.

"I'm not worried about your problems. I'm worried about what you might do."

The porch light leached color from his face. His fair complexion looked like ash.

"Tonight isn't your first visit, Will. You've been here before— the night you broke into the house."

No response.

I almost accused him of murder then. Told him that I knew, that I'd told the police too, so there was no point in continuing. But that would make him hurry. I wanted more time for someone to come.

He was quiet. Except for the weather that whipped grit from the driveway into our faces, we looked like we were casually visiting. I looked off into the early darkness and scanned the road for headlights. The police. Frank. Felix would be just fine. No lights. I was on my own.

I still had the lead. I kept my voice respectful, matter of fact. "You're an intelligent man."

Wind rattled the dry canes of the roses by the garage.

"Why were you after the film?" I said and answered my own question when he didn't. "You needed that oil pipeline to go through. You couldn't risk having it stopped because Bob dug up the graves."

"Bob was a funny guy." Will spoke at last. "If he put half the energy into a business as he did into this illegal archaeology, he'd have been a successful man. He was very professional about it, showed me the research he'd done at the University, the notes and measurements and pictures he'd made as he removed each piece."

"You told me you were a history buff yourself," I said, stretching out the conversation. "You must have been quite interested."

"Interested, but not stupid. I would never participate in an illicit dig. Too many people were watching the area. I was the one who encouraged him to close it up. But would he fill it back in with dirt? No. He wanted to be able to come back and see it."

"Neither of you thought about notifying the Snoqualmie Tribe?"

"Bob said it never occurred to him at first. Back East, you hear about farmers plowing up arrowheads all the time. They never notify anyone. By the time he realized the extent of what he had, it was too late. He'd waited too long and he couldn't let it go.

"As for me, no. Telling the tribe didn't seem advantageous. Better to avoid the hassle. It almost worked. In another few months, the undergrowth would have made it impossible to budge that brush pile without a backhoe."

"Martin never would have seen it when he went there to film."

"He'd be alive now," Will said and nodded with empathy. It felt manipulative. "Bob killed your friend to keep the film quiet. Martin confronted him about the dig. It was an accident. They struggled there at the river, Martin fell and hit his head. I was the only one Bob could talk to."

Maybe that story would convince someone who didn't know about Lydia's affair with Martin. Maybe I would believe it if I didn't know Martin had been bludgeoned. He was practicing his story on me; I knew he didn't care if I believed him.

Parts of it fit: the computer in Bob's truck, the trouble with the artifacts. Will looked convincing. He looked serious and concerned. But I knew he was an actor. I weighed the advantages of confronting him with the murder. But my rational thought had fled. All I could do was feel my way forward in the conversation. I couldn't see where I was headed.

"You left a nice swatch of that raincoat in the bushes after you broke into my house."

Will didn't veer. "Bob killed Martin to keep him quiet."

"What about Alfred Mallecke?"

He looked surprised and confused enough to make me question my assumptions.

"Ah, the homeless man." His expression became cloying again. "Bob Swan killed them both."

"Your motive is more believable—Lydia's affair. Maybe it was just like you said, an accident. Martin hit his head. But you killed Martin."

I raised my voice to be heard over the storm. A lull in the wind made the final words too loud. "You killed Martin," echoed in the clearing. Then the only sound was a drip from a rusted gutter joint. The intensity of my accusation startled him. For just a moment, his face was sad.

"It wasn't murder," he said. Anger took over. His eyes flicked left and right as he struggled for control. "As long as no one knew about the affair, I couldn't be connected. No one knew I had a reason."

"And Alfred Mallecke?" I didn't want his death to be invisible.

"The homeless man was just in the wrong place at the wrong time. He saw too much." Will swept the air dismissing the topic.

"Maybe Martin's death was accidental." I didn't believe that, but played along. "But you murdered Alfred Mallecke."

Will seemed to like having an audience and began to unwind the story. He wanted to talk. "I began to suspect Lydia of having an affair. She had evening meetings that lasted longer and longer, more errands that took her out of the house at night. She had a different smell, a different color about her." His voice was bitter. "She was in heat."

He looked toward the woods and Martin's house. "One night she said she was going to get groceries. I followed and damned if she didn't drive straight to the Safeway. For a minute, I thought I was wrong. Then she got into Martin's car and they drove away. I followed them out here, parked in that turnaround across the road, behind some trees. She stayed for hours."

I felt like his confessor as well as his next victim.

"I followed her for a week. She went almost every day, sometimes in the morning, sometimes at night." He came up from the memory and turned his cold green eyes on me. "There's a tail light out on your truck."

The change of attention unnerved me. Lydia's comings and goings weren't the only ones he watched. The wind picked up again and the two cedar trees that framed my house swayed in an unnatural dance. I wondered how long I could keep him talking. The drive from the police station in town took fifteen minutes. "What happened the day Martin died?" I prompted.

"I met Bob at the river to talk about Cathedral Falls. It was time he realized his fantasy was coming to an end. Bob was like a child. He bolted, saying he was going to talk to his father. I knew what Daddy would say. Well, on the way back to my car, I saw Martin Hanish there with the damned dog."

Will's eyes went past me to the long windows in the front door where Caesar stood. The puppy was young, but already stocky. He bared his teeth and growled. Will laughed.

"I meant to confront him. Frighten him. The man should have been contrite. But he insulted me, insulted my life. I grabbed the little asshole by his shirt and shook him. He was so small, so old. How could Lydia be with a man like that? I shook him and then I tossed him aside. He disgusted me. He fell."

Will seemed as unaware of the depth of his anger now as he must have been when he "tossed" Martin aside. His mouth pulled back in a grotesque expression.

"And Alfred Mallecke," I said.

"He saw it happen. He was as old and as slow as Martin."

"And the woman who was with Mallecke?" Liz wasn't old, but she was pregnant and probably slow.

"You know about her too? She ran. But I think she's too crazy to say what happened."

"How did you find her? You threatened her in the hospital."

"I found their things, a backpack and a couple of black plastic bags with blankets. Her name was there. Liz Larkin. I just called around the mental health centers and hospitals pretending to be a concerned family member. At Harborview, they wouldn't tell me if she was there, but they wanted to be helpful, you know. They transferred me to some patient phone where I could ask for her. Another patient went and got her right away. I had to scare her. It wasn't hard."

I shook my head and tried to understand the thinking that was behind what he had done.

"You don't like that? You're a do-gooder, Grace. You can't see those people for what they are. Throw-aways."

My fear tasted like metal in my throat. I had struggled to keep it at bay, but now I was too angry to be afraid. I hoped it would give me the strength to fight him.

"You're soft," he said, aware of the double entendre.

I didn't bother to respond.

"I'm not. I had to make a plan. I'd use Bob as a decoy. He would take the blame for Martin's death. The artifacts would be his motive. I took the computer and planted it at his house. I broke into your house to lead more suspicion his way." He clipped each sentence with an abrupt stop, the way I imagined him shaking Martin. My own anger was a dim reflection of his rage. That was fueled by the collapse of the rickety structure of the image he tried to project. There wasn't much left when it fell away.

"But why did you kill Bob?" I asked.

Will pushed his anger down again and stepped on to the porch. Close, his breath on my skin. "Let's say the opportunity presented itself. You're actually the first person I planned ahead of time to kill."

Chapter 29

WILL CROWDED ME, but didn't touch me. A sharp wind drove his scent into my face. He smelled of sweat and anxiety and I forced myself not to move away. I looked him in the eye and held him back with nothing more than my determination not to be intimidated. He stepped back instead.

"I've never had the opportunity for murder to present itself," I said. "You did. How was that?" I really wanted to know.

The porch light threw our shadows into relief, down the low step and onto the walk.

"Bob was a loose cannon," Will said. "Martin knew about his stupid archaeological game. The Indian did too."

"Felix George?"

"Yeah, the Indian. He threatened Bob. Bullied him. But all he wanted was to get everything back, the artifacts and especially the bones." Will shook his head back and forth as if he still couldn't believe it, as if murder were a lesser infraction. "Bob desecrated those graves and he was getting off scot-free."

"I talked to Bob every day that week—about Cathedral Falls, how the pipeline would benefit him too. It was easy money. But Bob fought it. He wanted a job. He saw himself as a quarry boss, a real workingman, not like his father, in business. When I went to see him Monday night—"

"The night you killed him."

Will ignored me. "He was in front of his trailer with Felix. They were puffed up and shouting. Bob decided to come clean about the dig—give everything back. Turn himself in to whatever authorities were in charge of protecting the graves. How noble.

"Felix said 'No" and grabbed him by the shirt front. He didn't want attention. Didn't want more people trekking up there to see what they could find. Felix left. Then I went in. But Bob wanted to put a stain on that property that would never come off. He was willing to crash and burn to do it. If his daddy wasn't going to let him have the quarry, Bob was going to make sure I didn't get the pipeline either. Bob acted like it was some kind of sibling rivalry—Dad picked me instead of him. It was just business," Will said. "The pipeline was better business."

"I guess it was more than business to Bob," I said. Will and Mr. Swan had a lot to do with the sibling rivalry issue. The night of the memorial, Will told me he would never forgive his own father, who gave him a bike, then hocked it to fuel his drinking. It must have seemed the same to Bob, who thought he'd finally forged a relationship with his father by working on the quarry with him. Then Mr. Swan took it away to fuel his thirst for business. Just business.

Will wasn't one to look at the situation from the other person's perspective. His eyes were untroubled by irony when he said, "I need that pipeline more than he needed the quarry. I need the money or I lose my wife, my home."

He went on with the story. "I didn't go there to kill him, but I couldn't reason with Bob. Then I got the most beautiful idea. No one had suspected me of killing Martin. I could do it again. I had seen that Mexican girl peeking out her door while Bob and Felix argued. She would think Felix killed Bob."

"She gave a statement to the police," I said. The story sickened me. "They took Felix in for questioning."

"The symmetry is quite elegant don't you think? Bob is blamed for Martin's death. The Indian is blamed for Bob's death. And soon for yours."

I finally got it. "You wrote the note telling Felix George to meet me. You planned it for this morning."

"The timing was thrown off when the police got to him, but he's free now. I think he'll come—or someone will think he did."

Will stepped close again, put his hand on my chin. My skin burned where he touched. "This will have to match Bob's murder. Don't you agree?"

The words brought back the knife and splattered blood where Bob lay in his trailer. I wondered if Will had a knife now or planned to use one of mine. My stomach lolled. My field of vision darkened around the edges. The disconnect of shock had protected me then. Not now. I had to think.

Will took hold of my wrist and jerked me toward the door. I drew back but his grasp tightened.

He didn't expect it. I was fast. I clasped both hands together like one big fist and swung my arms up. The momentum broke the circle of his grip. I had learned it at work in case a patient grabbed me. My arms flew up and I spun around until I was off the porch and Will fell backward into the door. The sound of breaking glass rang out. Caesar roared and leapt at the mullioned windows. The dog's gnashed teeth hit glass.

Will no longer stood between me and the truck. I ran.

Chapter 30

THE OLD DOOR CRACKED, wooden mullions splintered, glass in crumbled glazing crashed. And I ran.

Past Will's car. The lull in the storm ended. Cold rain, carried by a new gust of wind, stung my cheeks. My hip struck metal—the garbage cans spilled coffee grounds and rotten food to the ground in a slippery mess. I dug in my pocket for keys and glanced once as I jumped in the truck. In the inky darkness, Will sprawled on his back amid shards of glass. Where the door once held panes of window glass, the empty frames curved inward—a fractured grid backlit by the yellow lamps in the house.

"Get off me," he yelled.

Caesar, outside now, hung from Will's wrist, his jaw clamped and locked. A black stain of blood spread from one of them. Or both.

I jammed the key into the ignition, punched down the lock with my elbow and backed into the turnaround. Now the truck faced the house. Caesar had not let go. Will struggled toward me, dragging the dog with him, then pulled off the coat to free himself from Caesar's grip. The parka sleeve Caesar had gripped in his teeth was empty.

My tires spun on mud and loose gravel. Will jumped at the truck. His hands scrabbled at the door, searching for the handle. His face magnified in the window, inches from mine. But I looked straight ahead and peeled out of the driveway. A last glimpse showed Will on a sprint to his car.

I strained to see the yellow line where the pavement dropped away into the ditch. I had a minute's lead on him. His Mazda would be faster, handle better on the turns. My advantage was the thousand trips I'd made down this road, day and night in every kind of weather. I knew how fast to take the curves.

My truck shuddered, hit by a blast of wind. Branches cracked overhead. No headlights showed behind me, but the curves came often. I decided to lead Will straight to the police station in town and prayed someone would be there after six.

I slipped around the turns as fast as I dared. Cherry Valley Road straightened and dropped down to the intersection with Main Street. I was almost there. At the stop sign, I slowed, confused. The left-hand turn led to town, just a quarter mile now. But there were no lights. The houses, the businesses, the streets lay in darkness. The road stretched ahead black and silent.

A fallen tree blocked the road. The power line had come down with it. Town was dark and inaccessible, just steps away. Across the bridge, headlights snaked toward Main where deputies with illuminated wands waved the traffic away. Patrol cars were out in force. I couldn't reach them. I might have run on foot, but the electrical wire snapped and sparked across the road—alive.

I swerved right to Monroe. The way was straight and flat, easy to do sixty, or seventy if I wanted. But no lights came from that direction either. The road was black and empty.

Two miles flew by and Dorothy Miller's dairy barn hulked ahead. No electricity there. Cathedral Falls was to the right, always dark. I saw a bigger problem. The standing water that had covered the fields yesterday had risen. A flat fifty feet of water pooled across the road. I couldn't go on. I stomped on the brakes, unable to reach the Miller's barn.

The road disappeared into the flooded landscape. Black water stretched from the Cathedral Falls wetlands, over a low spot in the banked road, to the river. I couldn't judge the depth. In my rearview mirror, a set of headlights came into sight, maybe Will's. For lack of another choice, I drove ahead.

It didn't work.

Resistance took over. Water stopped the truck, swamped the engine, threw me forward into the steering wheel. The horn blared in my ears. I'd hit it. It stuck.

The car behind me sped closer. I threw open the door and stepped into the numbing flow. The shock of the icy water made me gasp. My jeans wicked the heavy water and made each step an effort. But I pushed into the current until the flood reached my thighs, my waist. Muddy ripples carried debris with me: branches, grasses, empty plastic bottles from someone's shed. Wind whipped the surface into choppy waves. The strength of the water tried to drag me off course, away from my goal, the Miller place.

The headlights from my stalled truck showed the best way to go. I pushed up to chest level and fought the surge of water that dragged at my saturated clothing, stiffened my limbs. I strained and dipped to avoid a wooden gate, broken pieces of a fence rushing toward me. The water was as dangerous to me as Will. It weakened me with cold. I fought for each step.

Then the water lowered. I was on my way out. I saw a flashlight swinging near the barn and screamed for help.

Maybe she'd heard the horn or seen the truck's lights. Dorothy Miller, in a slicker and barn boots, reached to help me out of the water. Her hold was strong. Rain streamed down her face. On the other side, Will jumped out of his car and stood at the edge of the flood.

"That's Will Taylor," I yelled through the wind. "He's the murderer." It probably sounded crazy, but Dorothy knew about Martin's death and heard my urgency.

She kept my hand in her tight, seventy-year-old grip and drew me into her barn. I felt protected and stumbled forward, my body weighted by wet clothing. Just inside hung a kerosene lantern, rusty enough to have lasted since before electricity came to the valley. Yellow light cast shadows of the Jerseys on the wall. Their udders were full after the power outage interrupted their automated milking. The warm smell of damp hides and manure seemed oddly comforting.

Dorothy guided me into a rough office and pointed to a shotgun over a metal desk. "I'm sorry," she said. "I never learned how to shoot. That was John's job." She pulled a box of shells from a drawer and spilled a couple into her hand. "You know how." It was a polite directive.

I reached for the gun. "My grandfather used to take me trap shooting. It's been years." I hefted the gun and worked open the barrel with stiff fingers.

Lantern light glinted in Dorothy's eyes. "You'll be fine, then."

"I wasn't bad," I said and placed shells in the double barrel.

We rushed back into the rain. I put my hand out. "You stay."

Dorothy turned to the barn. "I'll see if the phone is working."

Outside, the wind slapped wet strings of hair in my face. I pushed it out of my eyes and mouth and ran to the water's edge.

Will struggled at the middle of the wash, his movements slowed by the water. He was 30 yards away. I lined him up in the sight. I wondered if I really meant to shoot.

"Stop," I yelled into the wind.

Will inched forward with jerky movements. A light colored shirt plastered to his shoulders, his coat left behind with the puppy. At twenty yards, I shot. High and to the left on purpose. I got a reaction. Will jumped as the shot whizzed by. I had one more. Behind me, the wind howled through the barn and made the restless cows stomp and bellow. Will passed the deep center. He moved faster as the water gave less resistance. My headlights cast a weak beam at his back. I concentrated on the dark silhouette and then hoisted the shotgun again. My shoulder throbbed from the kickback from the last shot.

"Stop," I yelled again. "I'll aim for you next time." I knew he heard me.

Will pushed forward but veered from the course of my last shot, as if a second shell would follow the same course. The water was down to his hips, and he moved faster.

I squinted down the barrel. I had him in my sights. Did I want Will to stand trial or did I have to stop him now? I had to decide.

He fell.

In a long, disorienting moment, I realized what happened.

I never got the shot off. Will had swung away from my first shot at the road edge. He stepped into deeper, faster water and lost his footing.

I ran back into the water, to the brink where I guessed the ground fell away. I still shouldered the gun. Will floundered in moving water that drew him away.

"Help me." He grasped at the branch of a bush that looked too slender to hold him.

I stood ten yards from him. I stepped forward, checked for secure footing with each move. I didn't know if I would help. This was the man who thought less fortunate people were throwaways. And murdered because he thought his needs were more important.

A road sign that marked the speed limit was near him, securely planted in the water, close to where the shoulder dropped away.

"Try to make it to the sign," I called out. "The current is running that way."

Will didn't move from his branch. "I can't," he said.

I didn't trust him, but I inched closer. Water tugged at my legs and sucked away my strength. I reached the sign and clutched it. I considered the possibility that Will was luring me into danger. If I reached out to him, he could pull me in. Even if he didn't mean to, he might pull me under if the river was too strong. I hesitated; water sped by. He planned to kill me. A minute ago I was prepared to shoot.

"Please," he said. His voice lower, but close enough to hear.

I could almost reach him. But I didn't know if I could hold his weight in the current. I wrapped my numb fingers around the pole to test my grip. If he grabbed my hand and I couldn't hold on—if he didn't let go, he'd take me down with him. I hugged the signpost to my body.

"I won't hurt you. Don't let me go this way."

A flash of light reflected on the water. I turned to see the sheriff's car from Monroe speed to the water's edge. I had help. Will would be arrested.

The water ran black, its force invisible. Will's fair skin stood out against the darkness. Almost as impulsively as he must have shoved Martin to his death, I grabbed at a cedar board that floated toward me in the racing water and spanned the distance between us.

"Reach for the board."

Will stretched out his hand, two feet short.

"You have to let go of the bush to make it."

Will stretched again and pushed through the water toward the board. It jerked and splinters bit into my hand—he'd made contact. I clutched and held fast. The wood was a bridge between us.

He scrambled in the water, but his feet didn't catch.

"Kick like you're swimming."

He didn't advance.

"I can't pull you in," I yelled. "You have to save yourself."

Will lunged, his body arced above the surface; water rolled from his back in an icy sheet that refracted the beams from the Sheriff's headlights. He held the cedar board that connected us with one hand; his weight pulled through to my shoulder. I held fast to the sign post, wrapped arm and leg.

In slow motion, the man who meant to kill me reached. His free hand came from above like a swimmer's. Toward me. In the beam from my headlights, I saw a murderous look in his eyes. And I let go. The board that connected us fell away.

Without his weight at the other end, I swung back into the road sign. His reaching hand fell away and the force of the flood pulled him away without the connection. His feet lost the road beneath the surface and his pale moon face floated away. Will's dark shape moved downstream away from me. Tears coursed down my face.

Chapter 31

A BLANKET OF FOG settled around the house with a damp, morning chill. Frank and Nell were fixing the broken door, replacing it with a modern double-paned version. This door wouldn't leak cold air through the glass all winter. This door was sturdier and wouldn't be so easily broken by a man falling and a dog lunging against the old glass in rickety frames.

Caesar followed me upstairs. His head and shoulders were dotted with bald patches where the vet had shaved his fur to put in stitches. One cut missed his eye by a fraction of an inch. He had gone through the front door when I ran from Will that night. He had bought me enough time to get away. Caesar crawled under the bed and came out, one of my favorite shoes in his mouth. He presented it as a gift, the leather pocked with tooth marks. I removed the ruined shoe from his mouth and said "No." Gwen would be here later to take him home with her.

Four days had passed since the flood. It was time to repair the many kinds of damage left in its wake. When the water receded, the police called a search for Will. They found his body halfway to Monroe, tangled in a barbed-wire fence that had snagged him from the current. He wore a new, sheathed hunting knife attached to his belt. Carl Ring said the peaceful expression on Will's bloated face was a shock to him.

As far as I knew, Mr. Swan was biding his time before moving forward with whichever development he'd chosen for Cathedral Falls. He'd have to wait for all the fuss about the deaths to blow over. His son was dead. And Will Taylor, the man Mr. Swan thought would have been a better son, had killed him. Mr. Swan didn't have much luck with sons.

I visited Lydia two days later, another condolence call. I figured that, aside from the police, I was the only person who knew she was grieving the loss of two loves: Martin and Will. When I drove up to her house, a FOR SALE sign had already sprung up in the yard. All three garage doors were open, but only the Land Cruiser was parked there. The Mazda was out for body work, to repair the bullet holes.

Lydia had arranged a deal with the bank to avoid foreclosure, resigned her position with the county council and planned a move to Portland—where no one would know what happened. I asked if she thought she'd pursue any acting there. She said she had accepted an administrative position in the city government and had no plans to even visit a theater. I didn't stay long.

Today would provide another kind of closure. The Snoqualmie Tribe had invited me to a ceremony at Cathedral Falls to rebury their ancestors' bones. I layered a shirt and sweater over my jeans, then a rust-colored jacket and lug-soled boots, not the usual outfit for a burial. But this wasn't the usual burial.

I kissed Frank and Nell good-bye and started out.

~

The last song was sung, the last dance danced. Felix George wore a bright red cape that swirled and fell into folds with a clatter. Hundreds of hand-sewn buttons on a felt background rattled and caught the light when Felix moved. Cathedral Falls crashed in the background and the cold green smell of moss and rocks rose from the water. A knot of people huddled along the creek bank; families with toddlers, grandparents, and Liz, whose belly was so big she looked like she might give birth any minute. Young men jostled each other, embarrassed by the solemn occasion.

The archaeological dig that Bob had marked in perfect squares had been filled with the bones and covered with dirt and river rock. Members of the tribe decided to keep the carved artifacts he had unearthed. Those treasures would be displayed at a new tribal center and shared with future generations.

Felix spoke, "Our ancestors are at rest and we can be glad. Glad that through this time of death we have come to know them better and ourselves. Our children have touched the stones that the ancestors touched, seen this place where they walked and come to know their lives."

The sky lightened to a haze and the sun broke through. The last wisp of fog wove around the top of an old cedar somehow missed in a century and a half of logging. Most of the forest was deciduous, filled with weed-like alder that the ground used to ready itself for the next mature forest. Spaced between were giant stumps marked with notches where loggers had put in springboards to balance as they wielded the two-man crosscut saw.

The murder investigation had closed quickly after Will's death. All the bones and artifacts were released in a few days. The police had been discreet about Will's motives, but the media had a field day. Three murders solved. A secret plan for a gas pipeline revealed. And Indian bones.

Felix George talked to the press this time. I saw him on the six o'clock news, explaining the significance of the burial ground and what had been discovered. I was amazed—he'd been secretive so long. Then I laughed out loud when he told how to find the site. The directions would lead to an old fire lookout five miles northeast of Cathedral Falls, nowhere near the real burial ground.

When Felix finished talking, people began to file down the steep path one by one. Liz stood at the edge of the new grave. She wore a green cap over her hair and looked like a fairy queen who was eight months pregnant. I joined her there.

"The underground people are at rest," she said. It sounded perfectly normal under the circumstances.

"I thought you were crazy when you said that before."

"I was crazy." Liz grinned. Her cheeks were rosy from the hike to the falls, but dark circles under her eyes showed how tired she was. She looked sedated from the medication. She was also feeling the belated effect of weeks without sleep. Liz's movements were heavy and slow. People sometimes went through a period like this before they were fully stabilized. The right balance between psychotic energy and calm would come later. Her thoughts were more clear now. She'd be okay at home, but she had a few miles to go yet on her road to recovery.

"Crazy, but right." Liz looked at me sideways. "Everything seemed connected in some cosmic sense. But the pipeline explosion, the burial ground—they really were related. I was wrong about Felix though. He wasn't a murderer."

"No. Will Taylor went to a lot of trouble to make him look like one, though. I was afraid of Felix too. How are you feeling?" I asked.

"Not as scared as I was. I know you were scared too, but try feeling that way and being paranoid at the same time. People don't believe a thing you say." Liz's wool coat was buttoned at the throat but wouldn't close over her big belly. "Except you, Grace. I knew you listened. I'm better at sorting out what's real from what's delusional now. God, I hope the baby is okay. When I found out I was pregnant, I went off the medication—I didn't want it to hurt her. I hope I didn't hurt her anyway." She wove her hands together and supported her belly. "It's a girl, you know."

The woods around us were green in spite of the leafless undergrowth. Lichen covered the ground and crept up the tree trunks. Licorice fern sprouted from the crooks of mossy branches. I wanted to reassure Liz, tell her everything would be okay. But there was no way I could know. The odds were against her. The baby had a family history of mental illness on Liz's side, alcoholism on Leonard's side. At least this baby would be loved.

"Please make sure you take your medications," I told her. I wanted so badly for Liz to succeed. I almost offered to check in on her but caught myself.

"Don't worry," Liz said, as if she'd read my thoughts. "I'll be with Len. And the Department of Social and Health Services is going to send a caseworker twice a week after the baby is born. Richard is going back to law school, but their mother's burns are getting better. She's coming up to help."

She had her resources in place. Richard Black and his brother, Leonard, waited for us at the mouth of the trail. "Go ahead. I want to be alone for a minute." I put my arm around Liz and gave her a hug from the side. "You take good care of yourself."

"You too." She hugged me back and joined the line of people walking down the steep path. She placed each foot with care and kept her arms out for balance. Leonard walked with her to make sure she was okay.

Chapter 32

AT THE EDGE OF THE GRAVES, the newly turned earth smelled rich and fertile. The reinterred bones of the tribe's ancestors seemed to provide a connection with the future as well as the past. Even though a scattering of people remained at Cathedral Falls, the moment led to the quiet reflection I had avoided since the flood.

Everyone had told me to think about my mother, and it was still hard for me. I knew I had cared for her when she should have cared for me. I knew I equated that with love. I built my life around that caring and protecting—in some ways that was good. But, my efforts to protect reminded me of a time, as a girl, I'd found a baby bird that had fallen from its nest. I tried to intercede, to save it by wrapping it in cotton and feeding it with an eyedropper. But the bird died anyway. I had done the best I could, but sometimes there was no intervening in natural processes.

I had to accept the fact that I wasn't responsible for Alfred Mallecke's death. I had done the best I could in my evaluation but couldn't hold him. It wasn't his mental illness that killed him. I reached into my pocket and pulled out the broken statue that I had found in Alfred's belongings. He had carried the Virgin Mary with him for whatever solace she could provide.

I left the grave and walked to a rocky grotto in the hillside by Cathedral Falls, so close that a mist from the water swept my face in the slight breeze. There, I made a memorial to Alfred Mallecke with the Virgin and a prayer from me—in this place that had been considered sacred since the very beginning.

I had a harder time when I thought about Will Taylor. I could still feel the bite of the board that connected us that night in the flood, the weight of his body pulling me. I would never know if I could have saved him. The hopeful part of me still wanted to believe that if I had held on longer, he would have come ashore. And he wouldn't have killed me.

I blamed myself for his death—as much as I blamed him for the deaths of Martin, Alfred, and Bob. A part of me knew it wasn't the same. I hadn't killed him out of some narcissistic fear that my life couldn't withstand the truths I had to face. But that night, in the flood, I held his life briefly in my hands. And I let go.

Finding something to leave as a memorial for Will Taylor was harder still. I could have asked Lydia, but his belongings seemed hollow to me. This morning, I had thought about what would be meaningful to him. I looked around my house until my eyes rested on a small wire sculpture of a bicycle that a friend had brought from Africa. I thought Will would like it. He never got to keep the bicycle his father gave him. I placed it on another rock in the grotto and walked away.

I was the last one to leave the falls. I hiked out on the same path I'd taken the night Liz disappeared. Today, the fog lifted from the valley and left the sky blue and sparkling. The air warmed. I walked out of the forest onto the raised trail over the soggy fields. The flattened grass showed where the current had run in the flood.

At the highway, I could see as far as Dorothy Miller's barn. A dead salmon was stranded in the road where it had tried to cross with the flood. A clump of grass was snagged in the barbed wire fence where the water had carried it. Like Will had been. It would be a long time before I could travel this stretch of road without the flash of Will's face when I let go.

Clusters of people talked at the edge of the highway. Felix George, surrounded by a group of boys, still wore the ceremonial cape. The boys stood transfixed by a story he was telling. Felix broke away and came over. He studied me for a long time, his face ruddy and wrinkled under the white crew cut. Then he lightly touched my arm. "It's been a long week," he said. "Neither of us trusted each other. I'm sorry."

He surprised me. "I'm sorry too."

Felix pulled something out of his shirt pocket and placed it in my hand, a small package wrapped in leather. "I'd like you to have this."

"Thank you, but I couldn't—"

Felix stopped me. "Giving gifts is an important tradition." He reached out and closed my fingers around the packet. "Open it when you get home."

"Thank you," again, was all I could say. Then Felix smiled and turned back to the group of boys who waited.

~

The late afternoon sun glinted through the trees, just about to drop out of sight. Gwen's Volvo was parked in front of my house. I paused at the porch to admire Frank and Nell's carpentry. The new door was solid and swung without a hitch. We should have replaced it years ago. Caesar ran to meet me. He stayed by my knee as I walked in.

"Watch the dog," Frank called from the kitchen. "I let the chickens out to run."

Inside the wood stove pumped out too much heat. Once the fog burned off, the temperature must have topped sixty degrees, unseasonably warm. The windows were thrown open and fresh air cleared the rooms of winter stuffiness.

Gwen and Nell talked at the kitchen table while Frank fussed with dinner preparations. The scent of rosemary escaped when he opened the oven door to check the roasting chicken and vegetables. I gave him a kiss, poured myself some wine, and sank down at the table.

"How was the ceremony?" Gwen asked. She pushed a bowl of olives and French bread my way.

"Very moving." I told them about the burial, the songs, and the beauty of the day at the falls. The leather-wrapped package

Felix gave me was still in my pocket unopened. I had saved it to open at home, but now seemed like the wrong time. I waited for a private moment.

Caesar put his head in my lap and sighed as we talked. His eyes followed the path of my hand as I reached for a piece of bread.

Nell twirled her wine glass by the stem. She wore a tight t-shirt and jeweled cardigan that left a slice of tanned midriff showing above her jeans. "You're not really going to send Caesar home with Gwen, are you?"

"Oh yes, I am." I held an olive out for the puppy and he ate it, pit and all.

"You sure?" Gwen looked at the young husky with his stitched up hide. He rested his warm head on my knee again. "That dog saved your life."

"We need a puppy around the house again," Frank said from the stove.

Nell tossed Caesar a corner of bread that he caught from his place at my knee. He knew which one of us he had to convince. Nell shot me a knowing smile. "You need someone to take care of, Mom. You should keep him."

Everyone looked at Caesar.

I paused and pretended to be unconvinced.

Then I ruffled an unshaven spot on the puppy's head. "All right. I guess he can stay. The dog and the chickens can take turns going outside."

The light began to fade as we talked. Supper was almost ready, so I excused myself to put the chickens in. Outside, I set my wine glass on the porch railing and watched the littlest hen chase the gnats that came with the warm weather. I finally pulled Felix's leather package out of my pocket and untied the string that held it together.

The flat, carved rock fit my palm. Chiseled lines followed the natural contours of the stone, a woman's face, stylized with large eyes in concentric circles. Felix had enclosed a paper that read, "A guardian spirit to watch over you, as you watched over

Liz and her baby." A light breeze blew in as the evening cooled. I blinked back tears and cupped my hands around the carving, still warm from my pocket.

In the dusky clearing, the chickens headed back to roost. I followed to secure the coop for the night and waited for all the girls to file in but didn't see the rooster. I found him perched on an old stump at the edge of the woods, proud, still missing his tail. The rooster puffed and preened his glossy red feathers. Then he threw back his head and crowed—even though it was the wrong time of day.

Acknowledgments

Writing a first novel, from "I think I can" to completion, has been an amazing process. By far, writing these acknowledgements will be the most rewarding because so many people have helped and supported me.

First, I must recognize my writing mentor, Waverly Fitzgerald, who has taken me from first draft to publication. Her knowledge, encouragement, and more than that, her example of how to make writing a way of life are an inspiration. There aren't enough ways to thank you.

Two writing groups helped me wrestle my words into submission. My Friday morning writing group, Linda Anderson, Rachel Bukey, Hannah Palin and Janis Wildy, listened patiently to each chapter and were always spot-on with feedback. They (Curt Colbert included) even allowed me to come back after a long absence. Another group, the Renton Writers—especially Theresa Zimmerman and Mary Brockway—also helped form my writing.

I owe Malice Domestic, the annual conference celebrating the traditional mystery, a great thank you for the vote of confidence in awarding me a grant for unpublished writers. More thanks go to Catherine Smith for careful editing and to Marlee Darrock for her extraordinary work with the final proof.

Ray Mullen of the Snoqualmie Tribe and JR Akey of the Duvall Police Department were generous in answering questions. All mistakes are mine. Even more thanks to Jean LaPaze and Jim Vail who kindly looked at my earliest chapters when I most needed encouragement to just keep going.

My husband, Jim Limardi, is the best supporter I can imagine. He tirelessly talked plot points over wine, then read each word in each revision twice—or more. Thanks for having read and watched so much noir, Jim. Eli Limardi deserves a prize for starting out a teenager and managing to grow into such a sweet man over those years.

Last, but not least, thank you to my friends and patients at Harborview Medical Center—which is truly the compassionate heart of Seattle.

About the Author

MARTHA CRITES has worked in community and inpatient mental health for twenty years and taught at the Quileute Tribal School on the Washington coast. She lives with her husband in Seattle. When she isn't working and writing, you will find her walking or volunteering on the Camino de Santiago in Spain.

Please visit her at www.marthacrites.com.

Other mysteries set in Seattle

from Rat City Publishing

Leap of Faith
By Rachel Bukey
  Seattle Times reporter Ann Dexter is always on the hunt for the big story—the one that will catapult her from beat reporter to the Pulitzer Prize. When a wealthy widow jumps to her death from Seattle's suicide bridge, leaving all her money to a sketchy new age church and its resident psychic medium, Ann is intent on exposing the psychic as a fraud, yet she can't deny the truth in the messages he brings from her loved ones. Ann's search for answers brings her face to face with a twisted killer and challenges all of her beliefs about love and life and death.
  978-09835714-5-7

Rat City
By Curt Colbert
  Jake Rossiter, a WWII vet and hard-boiled PI, tracks down a killer with help from his girl Friday, Miss Jenkins, in this historical novel set in Seattle in 1947. The noir atmosphere is thick as Rossiter tangles with corrupt cops and dangerous dames, in jazz clubs and on the Seattle docks, at a swanky downtown department store, and in a deserted amusement park. A Shamus Award Nominee for Best First PI Novel.
  978-09835714-0-7

www.RatCityPublishing.com

CPSIA information can be obtained at www.ICGtesting.com
Printed in the USA
LVOW07s2135040216

473776LV00003B/209/P